FRANK ROSS

BANK ROBBER DAMES

PX DUKE

FRANK ROSS

BANK ROBBER DAMES

Bank Robber Dames

The road never ends. Neither does the adventure.

Fast Company

The first time I laid eyes on her we were in some hick town. I needed a break from the sweltering heat and the dust on the two-lane blacktop I had been riding since early morning. I pulled off and parked on the outside end of a row of cars closest to the highway.

After I shut down, I could hear the loud pipes rumbling past on the highway. I focused my gaze on the motorcycle as it pulled in, one building down from where I stopped.

The rider parked in an outside slot at the gas-n-go. That's where I liked to be when I wasn't hiding out. With nothing else close by, it made it easy to keep an eye on things when the lookie-loos got nosy.

She leaned the bike over, removed her helmet, and looked around. I knew the woman had seen me and my ride, because she stopped mid-look for an instant too long before her gaze moved on.

I watched her strike out across the lot toward the stop-and-puke. She was tall and slim and long-legged and walked with an attitude. Like she knew where she was going and what she was doing.

She swung her head one more time to take another look before she got to the door. My eyes remained locked onto her, and she must have known by now.

I nodded through the distance between us.

She acknowledged and kept on toward the joint to push through the door.

I was never shy about checking out a woman who rides. Some liked it. Some didn't. I pretty much ignored the ones that didn't, and left them alone.

I needed food. A bowl of soup and a grilled cheese was quick. The sandwich shop offers that, and I sat in front of the window to keep an eye out while I waited.

Half-way through my soup, she re-appeared and retraced her path across the lot with that same purposeful stride. She had a couple of water bottles dangling from one hand. When she got to the bike, she unscrewed a cap and chugged one. The other she tucked into a leather saddlebag.

Smart move in this heat.

It was obvious she'd been down the road more than a mile or two. The woman saddled up and headed on down the road in the same direction I was headed.

I considered hurrying off to join her.

I didn't. Instead, I took the time to finish my soup.

Did I mention I like soup? It's a daily special in a lot of diners. No waiting, either. They give it a stir and ladle it out of a pot into a bowl.

When next we crossed paths, she was only a mile or so ahead.

Okay, so I had to ride like hell to get there, but she wasn't exactly going as fast as that either. That was why it was so easy to catch up.

I closed the distance and trailed her for a few miles. She slowed even more and allowed me to come up behind her. I figured it was intentional when she moved from the middle of the lane to the left. I pulled in beside her in the right track.

We danced like that for a while.

Flying in formation.

Side-by-side down the highway.

Easy when both knew how to ride and could hold steady speed.

A lot of riders can't. They're the reasons biker women check out the boots first. New boots are a dead giveaway.

Eventually she dropped back in her track and held steady half a length behind me.

I kept an eye on her in the mirror, and let her take the opportunity to have a closer look at what she might be getting herself into.

I let her check. Evaluate. Is this one okay?

How is he sitting? Relaxed? Tense? How is he dressed? RUB? Biker?

She took her time and she must have been satisfied, because she pulled ahead for half a length. That allowed me to get a better look at her, too.

I already knew I liked what I saw.

She rode a black Softail. It was covered in plenty of grime, just like my bagger. For sure we had been on the road in the same weather.

She sat behind a windshield. None but the dwindling greybeards put on the miles without one. Her ride was piled high with bags. I spotted a tent, too. A second helmet, full-face, hung off the back. Some like to wear one when the rain proved to be steady.

She was dressed in dark brown and black. Her boots were laced high and looked well worn.

Tribal tattoos ran up and down her bare arms and neck, probably all over. A small nose ring decorated her face.

She had seen lots of sun.

Early thirties. Maybe pushing late thirties at the very most. No girl on a motorcycle, this. She was pure riding woman.

I pulled ahead a few lengths and held steady for three or four miles, giving her the option to catch up.

She did.

When she went by, she arced toward me and then pulled back and slightly ahead. That's the sign I was waiting for. I pulled in close beside her and we flew in formation for a hundred miles, positioning back and forth.

I had the feeling that we were doing a dance. That, and we were easy company for each other on the lonely road when both knew how to ride.

Eventually, city lights grew closer. We ended up riding side-by-side through the busy streets. In the corners she was on the inside for some, me on the outside for some. We kept side-by-side. It was easy now. We had practiced doing exactly the same for over a hundred miles on two-lane blacktop.

All that highway riding hadn't given us a chance to talk.

When changing lights interrupted our dance, we continued sizing each other up, this time with questions we hadn't had a chance to ask.

Traffic backed up behind us. We ignored it and carried on talking, oblivious to the four-wheeled cages filled with bored occupants.

We didn't care. We were still dancing, circling, coming back to one another.

"Where are you headed, chica?"

"Where are you from?"

"You put a lot of miles on that thing?"

"Are you running from or running to?"

That was always my question.

t got a grin, because she knew exactly what I meant, and when she nodded, I knew exactly what she meant.

I returned the grin and nodded back.

We had it finally figured out that we were both drifting, and we grinned together. Like we were looking into the same mirror. Then she told me where she'd be camping out for the night.

I knew the place. I had ridden past it many times on my way around the north shore. It was past the city and north, by five or ten miles. I broke off and took on fuel. With a full tank, I headed north.

She was in the film industry in California. I was just back from there. I had no plans to re-visit. When I thought I should have, it was too late.

Sometimes, the road is lonely.

Sometimes, it isn't.

Searching for Jennifer

The **woman appeared in** the velvety darkness of night. Like an apparition. Alone. Dressed in black. Almost invisible but for the long shadow cast by the headlights pouring light around her.

But for that, I would never have noticed her.

Who was she?

Where was she going?

Why was she alone in the night?

Perhaps someone thought she was little more than window dressing and dumped her on the curb in the middle of nowhere.

I knew all about nowhere.

I've been there a time or two.

I pulled up beside her and rolled down the window. "Get in," I commanded through the opening.

She stood up, exhaled a cloud of smoke, and flicked her cigarette to the ground before picking up her bag. Without so much as a word, she opened the door, climbed in and tossed the bag over the seat into the back. It barely made a sound landing on the seat.

I remember thinking there couldn't be much in it.

She sat with half of her back on the seat. The other half leaned against the door. Wary. It allowed her to keep an eye on the road and one on me.

I didn't say anything. I figured she'd talk when she wanted to. After a couple of miles, I finally gave up.

"Going anywhere?"

"Yes, I am. As far away from here as I can get," she replied.

That was my cue to keep the car pointed in the direction of the four-lane and headed for the open road.

I tuned the radio to some mellow 40s music and lost myself in the cigarette-and-whiskey-coated voice drifting up from the speakers.

From time to time, I looked across at her.

Her eyes were closed. Her breathing was regular. She was fast asleep. Her head tipped and rested against the seat-back. Long, dark hair spilled over her shoulders.

I let her sleep.

Next stop, gas, and a hundred miles later I went in to pay.

When I returned to the car, she was just getting out. Her bag was on her lap.

She saw me, sat back down, and looked up.

"Where are we?"

"About a hundred miles from nowhere. You slept all the way," I said. "You passed out almost as soon as the door closed."

"Yeah, I was beat. I needed sleep," she said. "Where are you going?"

"Anywhere but here," I said, grinning.

"I'm with you." She turned in the seat and closed the door. "Let's go."

She put her feet up on the dash and pushed back into the seat.

For some reason, I was glad she was making herself at home. I liked that.

"Mind if I smoke?" she asked.

"No, go ahead."

She pulled a pack of Marlboros from her jean-jacket pocket and bumped a cigarette between her fingers. "You want one?"

"No thanks."

She flicked a wooden match alive with a quick flick of her thumb.

"Where did you learn to do that?"

"What? The match trick? Some guy in a club I used to work in showed me."

"A club? You're a dancer."

"Was," she replied. "Not any more."

That's all I managed to get out of her. I had my own secrets, so I let it go and pretended to concentrate on driving.

When I looked across at her again, her eyes were closed. Smoke drifted out of the half-open window from the still-burning cigarette clutched in her hand. I reached for it and slipped it from between her fingers before tossing it out the window.

Either I bored the hell out of her or she was dead tired.

I turned off the radio and put on some Nina Simone. If she didn't like my music, she was in the wrong place.

A few minutes later, she woke with a start and looked across at me.

"Bad dream?" I asked.

"Sort of. You ever have one?"

"Not for about the last two hundred miles. Why? Do you have them a lot?"

"I have plenty of shit going on in my life right now," she said.

"I hear that," I said, and didn't ask any questions. "You didn't tell me your name."

"I'm Jennifer."

"Well, Jennifer, I'm glad we ran into each other. I'm Frank."

We passed the occasional dim light in the distance on one side of the highway or another. Single houses, probably. Set well back from the road.

Sometimes there were clusters of lights.

Jennifer turned to gaze after them as they went by in the night.

"Ever wonder what it would be like to settle down into one of those places?" I asked.

"Sometimes. Not for long. You?"

"I tried it for a while. Always something else coming at you out of nowhere. More bills to pay. Furniture to buy. Keeping up with the neighbors. I got tired of it all after a while. It sounds like you did, too."

She didn't answer, and instead kept staring out the side window into the night.

"There's a truck stop a few miles down the road where the interstate crosses this one. I'll be stopping for gas and coffee."

"Sure," she acknowledged.

Twenty minutes later, I took the exit and turned into the white-light jungle of gas pumps and parked semis.

I fueled and tried to pay at the pump but it wouldn't take my card. I went in to pay and returned to the car.

It was empty.

Jennifer was gone.

Disappeared.

I waited a few minutes at the pumps, then parked under a light and went to the restaurant for a cup of coffee and a bowl of soup.

Thirty minutes later she still hadn't shown, so I wandered back to the car.

Beneath a wiper blade, a piece of paper waved in the breeze. I hadn't seen it earlier because it wasn't there.

Thanks for the miles between here and there, Frank. Maybe I'll see you again sometime. Jennifer

Well now, that was short and sweet.

I wondered where the line *Anywhere but here* would get her in a place like this.

Daylight was beginning to slowly break in the east. It was time to go.

I pointed the car south. Before I turned onto the interstate, I looked over my shoulder. A dark shape lay draped across the back seat.

I pulled over and stopped to take a better look.

It was Jennifer's bag.

No name tag. No wallet. No credit card receipts. There was nothing but a manila envelope containing a stack of photographs. All of them of Jennifer. All in black and white.

They appeared to be professionally done. Portfolio quality. Taken in a loft. She looked pretty good, too. Nude, but not nude if you get the idea. Arms and long hair covered the strategic parts.

I was never able to return the photos to her. There was no ID in the bag.

If you see her out there, tell her I'm looking for her.

I'd like to return the photographs.

Epilogue

Jennifer called from a pay phone in Nara Visa a few days ago. How she got my number I'll never know. She thanked me for picking her up and getting her out of town.

She told me she had to get far away in a hurry. She apologized for running off at the truck stop, but it couldn't be avoided, she told me.

"Nothing personal, you understand," she said.

I understood all right and just listened.

I didn't ask questions. I barely knew her, and I certainly didn't need any more heartache in my life. Somehow, I knew she'd be capable of giving me a belly-full.

Sometimes, I can tell that about a woman. More often, I can't.

She hung up, and I got back in the car and headed west.

Life is good out there.

So I hear.

Crazy Eyes

I was running hard in the early morning. The sun was at my back.

I was headed west on the 10.

My day started long before that. Hours earlier in the dark of night, I was out of Roswell—where the day before had been hot and dry, just like all the others before it—and through Alamogordo and Las Cruces. I wanted to escape the heat I knew would be setting in for the better part of the day before much longer.

Thankfully, it stayed cool into the early morning, but experience said it wasn't going to remain that way forever.

I grabbed a tankful in Deming, and that got me into Willcox at around eight in the morning, perhaps eight-thirty.

Maybe a little later.

It was still cool, but with the sun getting higher, it looked more and more like it would be turning into another scorcher. The still, hazy air had that look. It was the look that said it would get hotter than hell before much longer.

I pulled off the 10 into a gas-n-go and did a quick turnaround. That meant get gas, get water and get out.

I backtracked and climbed the overpass that would take me back to the 10, westbound, one more time.

On the top of the overpass, someone was standing on that narrow concrete walkway, leaning against the railing. Whoever it was had on one of those generic green parkas to keep warm against the cool in the desert morning. A small bag dangled from one shoulder.

In the split second when I recognized the someone to be a woman, I hit both brakes hard and pulled off onto the shoulder.

I figured I had room for one more. I could strap the bag onto the trunk to make rear-seat room and be back on the road post-haste.

I didn't circle around. In that split-second when I decided I wanted to take my time and investigate, I shut down, climbed off, and waited for her to catch up.

She was wearing dark glasses. It was impossible to see her eyes through the tinted lenses. I like to be able to see their eyes if they're going to be throwing a leg over. It's a little peeve I have about women and eyes.

I don't like crazy eyes. For me, crazy eyes always spelled trouble. Trouble meant she wouldn't remove her dark glasses.

With no eyes to go by, I figured I'd evaluate

the rest of her.

Just in case.

A multi-colored scarf shielded her head against the climbing sun. She was bundled up against the fresh morning air in an old, dark-green army parka. Dark socks and sandals covered her feet.

The bag hanging off her shoulder turned out to be mesh. It looked to be filled with mail, or letters, or perhaps documents of some sort.

Dressed as she was, I took her for a local, probably trying to hitch her way back to town. She had to be. There were no buses on the road.

Funny thing, though. I didn't see anyone on the overpass when I crossed it the first time. I saw no one walking away from the store when I pulled in.

I didn't ask questions. Instead, I pushed my sunglasses onto the top of my head, hoping she would do the same.

Like I said, I wanted to get a look at her eyes.

No such luck. She didn't take the hint. She kept them on and revealed nothing.

She said her name was Angel. She was headed west for a bit, then north to a music festival, of all things, she said.

Well now, I figured I could use some entertainment. And it's Friday. I don't need to be in Phoenix until Monday. Why not take a detour and check out the sights and sounds? I might even have a guide.

"No problem," I told her. "I'm going that way."

What the hell, I had a full tank of gas and I didn't need to be anywhere.

Angel climbed on and I headed off to a music festival.

Out there somewhere.

She showed me where to pull off the 10 to connect with the route to the festival. I don't remember the exact exit, but I'm certain it was well before Benson, and probably by Johnson.

Eventually, the two-lane blacktop changed direction from north to west.

Now, I'm a gullible bastard when it comes to women, but I try to keep one eye open. For a music festival trail, this road was remarkably free of traffic, notwithstanding its closeness to Tucson. In fact, I didn't see any other traffic.

None at all.

I mentioned that to Angel.

"Maybe I got the day wrong," she said into my ear.

The hair on the back of my neck started to twitch just a bit.

Let's see if I had this right. I was in the middle of nowhere, having swallowed lock, stock and two smoking barrels, a music festival storyline that started to look and sound more and more like a fairy tale. The woman on the back had her days mixed up. There was no word on where I was really headed or what might be waiting for me at the end of the trail.

Adventurous as I was, this was starting to get a little weird. I never did like riding into rabbit-holes, even though I've managed to end up in a few.

Not willingly, of course.

Another thirty or forty isolated miles went by before I happily crossed paths with a small country store. I was somewhere, finally, and it was past time to pull off the road. The pavement ended there, and the gravel road ahead rose toward low hills in the distance.

I explained to Angel that I couldn't take my heavy decker onto gravel and made my apologies.

That's not the truth, of course. I've ridden on plenty of gravel. I thought it a prudent story to go with at the time.

Angel appeared happy to be anywhere, so I said goodbye and left her walking toward the store.

I backtracked on the music festival road to nowhere, hit the 10 where I exited with Angel, and headed on into Phoenix.

In retrospect, I'm sure Angel wanted only to get as close to her destination as she could. Selling a story about a music festival to a stranger riding through on a motorcycle probably seemed the easiest way to do that.

I'd have preferred the truth, of course, and would have been happy to take her to where she wanted to be if only she had told me so.

I never did get to see her eyes.

Marked by Life

I was stopped in Grand Forks. At least, that's what the sign told me. I had no idea how many miles of four-lane flat-top I left in the rearview. Exhausted as I was, I still knew what day it was.

Saturday.

Not that it was important.

Or that it mattered.

I had started out before sunup when the early morning air was still cool. As the day wore on, it got a whole lot hotter. I had burned no daylight to get here, and now it was getting on in late afternoon. The sun might have been lower in the sky, but the heat that built during the day hadn't dissipated in the slightest. I'd find little relief when I rode on into the darkness of night.

Heat and distance having gotten the better of me, I sought refuge in the shade at a gas-n-go and drank water to keep hydrated. I needed the break from the day's relentless sun and hot, dry wind.

I needed to stretch my legs, too.

All day on a motorcycle will do that. Coming out of the southern high desert and riding hard through the heat across the Great Plains will make it worse. I wasn't ready for the hundred-and-a-half I still needed to do to get home. It was only another couple of hours, but all I wanted to do was stop right here.

What I needed was an excuse.

Any excuse.

That's why I was so interested in the beater shaking and rattling across the parking lot in the direction of the air pump against the wall. The windows were down. Obviously, the air conditioning wasn't doing its duty—if it was even working.

Rusty hinges squeaked when the driver forced the door open and closed. My attention was no longer on the heat. It was all on the woman who got out. She was young. Maybe mid to late twenties at the most. Pretty, too, in a plain sort of way.

Her hair was dark—my nemesis. Dark hair and dark eyes had a habit of always getting in my way if I wasn't afraid to let it.

Most of the time, I let it. Not always, though.

Both sleeves on the white shirt the woman was wearing were neatly rolled up against the heat. Bare arms halted just above her elbows.

Well-worn brown shoes matched dark brown slacks.

I figured she was probably on her way to start her shift as a bartender or a waiter.

She made a grab for the air hose and stooped

to fill the left front tire. She couldn't quite get it to take air.

The perfect gentleman I am, I saw opportunity.

I ambled over and offered to help.

She explained she was on her way to a wedding reception and was running late.

She handed me the hose, and I took it.

In her haste to get to work, she must have forgotten about those rolled-up sleeves. As she stood and handed over the hose, I saw the track marks running the length of both forearms. They were healed over and scarred—definitely not fresh by a long shot.

From of the corner of my eye I could tell she saw me notice the scars.

I looked up at her. "Are you all right?"

It was the best I could offer under the circumstances.

She smiled. "I am now."

I finished what I volunteered to do. The woman thanked me and the door squeaked again and closed and she drove off.

I saddled up and rode the rest of the way home in the heat.

I was just happy to be there.

Truck Stop

Iwas living in southern California at the time.

I met her at a truck stop in Ontario. She was from the northeast. Maine, if I remember right. Not your usual highway habitué.

She drove a truck. A semi. A tractor-trailer.

Through snow. Ice. Rain. Fog.

Eighty thousand pounds of metal rolling on rubber through a never-ending litany of towns, cities and truck stops. Along multi-lane expressways. Down interstate highways. Over two-lane blacktop.

Past Chicago.

Atlanta.

Birmingham.

Pecos.

Los Angeles.

Across a table from one another, we shared stories of riding and of driving and of the road. Stories of characters met. Of people seen. Places to eat. Things heard.

Stories of loneliness.

Then it was time to go. We both had to get back on the road.

"I'll call," she said. "The next time I get to California."

She called one time, and I rode out to meet her.

She called again, and I rode back to love her.

She doesn't call any more.

Midnight at the Oasis

Part 1

The desert fan palm is the largest palm tree in North America. It can grow to a height of 75 feet. Trunk diameter can be up to three feet. Its leaves can grow on the stalk to over six feet in length. Extremely sharp spines on the leaf's two edges are capable of cutting skin very badly. When the leaf dies it remains attached throughout the life of the tree. A skirt of dead leaves can build up, completely obscuring the tree trunk. Strong winds can blow these dead leaves off. Fire is also known to burn off the dead leaf stem.

New Growth

My day began in the cool morning air of the low desert. It didn't stay that way for long. Only a bit later the heat became unbearable for a northerner like me. The gas-n-go stops, where nary a whisper of a breeze penetrated, were only a little better for the air conditioning within and the ice-cold water that made up for a lack of shade.

A fresh tank of gas got me back into the heat and headed north on the 10. I was bound for the high desert. Climbing the three thousand feet of elevation revealed nightfall's freezing cold desert air. As though to make up for the crazy temperature swing, an almost full moon beamed down in a cold, white glare. In a few days the moon would be full. In those few days, I planned on being a lot farther south where I'm hoping for a more even warmth.

It was time to get off the road, climb off the motorcycle and get out of the high-desert cold. I needed to hug some warmth for a day or two, at least. I pulled into an old desert inn I heard about some months ago. I checked in, got a key, and was directed to the last cabin in the row. It was all by itself. Just the way I liked things to be. I'm shrouded in darkness, alone and isolated.

I unlocked the door and pushed it open. The heavy wooden door creaked on giant hinges. Fierce moonlight streamed through a window with open curtains, revealing the cabin's interior. I couldn't find the light switch—no big deal with the natural light in the room anyway. In any case, I'm too exhausted by too many miles to care.

I walked out to my ride and unloaded a bag

from the trunk. It's all I needed, and in any case, I'm too tired to want to do anything but hit the sheets.

I crashed into bed and slept as though dead.

A new day's morning sun rose, warm and inviting. I chose to enjoy it by the pool next to the restaurant. The pool is sheltered from the view of passers-by with a high wall. I took up a chair overlooking it. I watched. Pretended not to watch. Tried to watch and not be noticed.

The swimmer's bathing suit appeared to be matched to the exact color of the pool. The color forced arms and shoulders and legs to appear as though disconnected from the rest of her body. This disconnection was the first thing I noticed, and wondered if the woman bought the one-piece for just that effect.

The swimmer moved closer to the edge of the pool, approaching. Long red hair was slicked back as she moved through the water. Freckles glistened on her face through the watery sheen.

At first it was her eyes that drew me. Their green was intensified by the shading of the pool. The show of disconnected arms and legs didn't hurt, either.

"Hello." The swimmer smiled tentatively. Hands moved to sweep water from her face.

I answered her. "Hello."

Long, slender fingers reached to slick her hair behind her ears. It was a useless movement when she pushed off to begin again her slow, languid laps. The water barely rippled as she passed back and forth in front of me. With each length traveled, she eased closer.

Finally, she halted in front of me again. She pushed up and her shoulders are just out of the water. Her red hair spread in an arc behind her. It resembled a dark halo. Again she brushed errant hair behind her ears. This time, she raised both elbows high, arching her back. Her breasts pushed forward.

I liked it when they showed off.

It was no longer green eyes that kept me transfixed. Breasts also begged for attention and admiration.

I stopped pretending and made sure she saw me flick my eyes over her. She recognized the look and smiled. She had my attention. She recognized I could no longer ignore her. She knew my true purpose. Perhaps I knew hers, too.

The dance was beginning.

She swam closer and halted, fumbling with her wet hair. She rested her elbows on the edge of the pool. Crossed her arms beneath her breasts. They swelled gently upwards, framed by the crossed arms beneath. She smiled. I took it as tacit approval to look. She wasn't shy, this one.

"Where are you from," she wanted to know. Still smiling.

Intent on the picture, I was caught unaware. I blurted a response and hope I wasn't being too obvious, yet I know I am.

She smiled once more. I smiled back. And then she pushed off and went back to her laps. Her legs kicked and water splashed and she is gone. She glided, noiseless, under water. Hands and arms pulled. Feet and long legs kicked. The surface distorted, rippled, her body shimmered and danced beneath the surface.

I watched, intent. No longer pretended. It's what she wanted me to do.

Again, she stopped to rest in front of me. Again she hovered with her breasts out of water. Hands pass back over her hair and down across her face with the same result as before. There is the hint of a smile again.

I smile back.

"Have you been here long?" she asked.

"Since yesterday. And you?" I prayed silently. Let her be a guest at the inn. I wanted to dance, too.

"I work here."

Inwardly, I release a sigh. The day has started to look considerably brighter.

She pushed off again and went back to her laps, but now they are no longer laps. She has committed to a different kind of dance. She is under the water and leaping out of the water with legs that kicked and thrashed and splashed. One lap. Another. Then she slowed abruptly and climbed out at the far end of the pool.

She bent to pick up her towel. Threw it carelessly across her shoulders. Tossed her hair while looking across at me. She waved, carefully, it seems.

Yes, swimmer, I see you. I am paying attention. I have been all along.

I wave back. The show is over. The dance is complete.

For now.

My adobe cabin is far from the main building and the pool. It's the last one on a long and winding dirt trail. Last night my headlight helped lead me past desert cholla to the gate at the end of the narrow trail. Cholla is a spiky trap for the unwary in the dark of night.

Once at the cabin, a creaky wooden gate bars entrance to a small courtyard containing two dusty chairs. They sat at a makeshift table cut from a palm tree's huge trunk .

A thick, heavy wooden door guarded entrance to my room. It hangs off a sturdy frame by means of three huge, black steel hinges that creak when the door is opened. A steel latch keeps it closed and secured against all adventure. It appeared strong enough to keep out an army.

I named the place Fort Apache, and felt

secure once inside.

The room looked to be typical desert fare, once common in the 50s or perhaps even earlier. There's a fireplace to enjoy and a leather chair in front of it to sit and stay warm while doing so. I'm content knowing I'll be comfortable here, and safe. If someone wants in, they'll have a pretty tough door to breach before they can get to me.

I don't anticipate a chance of that happening.

The cabin will be home for at least a couple of days. Maybe more. After riding hard through the cold to get here, I wanted to catch my breath and warm up a bit before I decide on the route I will take in search of warm-weather adventure. Eventually, I will head south, down Mexico way.

There is nothing to hold me here.

Somehow, I managed to miss lunch. Dinner is still hours away. To kill time, I wandered the grounds. Stacks of firewood leaned against an outbuilding. I knew where I would get wood for tonight's fire in my adobe fireplace.

Old palm trees with trunks shrouded in dead leaves shade a small pool of stagnant water. The inn's location must have been chosen because of it, and the adobe look of the cabins confirmed it. In its prime, the old drive-in motel would have been a veritable oasis in the middle of a hot, high-desert summer of nowhere.

Walking the grounds hasn't sated my appetite for more of the morning's poolside apparition. What passes for food in the restaurant will feed my more immediate appetite. It won't satisfy my hunger for more of the woman. I'm even more eager to see her again.

I want to know if she will continue the dance.

I end up sitting at the bar. It's where I want to be, with my back to the wall. Waiting. Watching. Enduring disappointment.

In my dismay, I finished my Sol and order dinner, thinking I won't get to see her tonight. It's a huge frustration after witnessing the performance in the pool. After all, she told me she works here. Perhaps during the lunch crowd I missed earlier—

Halfway through dinner, my reward arrived when the swimmer came in from the kitchen and walked directly toward me. Still smiling. I mirror her smile, for I am grateful for the sight of her. I can't help it.

"I'm Rachael. From this afternoon by the pool, remember? Hello again."

Not shy, this one, but I already knew that. And yes, I remembered. How could I forget the performance so soon?

"I'm Frank. It's a pleasure to finally meet you, Rachael. I was hoping I'd see you again," I said. Why not be obvious? "Will you sit down and join me?"

"I can't stay long. I'm working," Rachael informed me.

"So late?"

"A relative owns the place. I work for her."

"Then you must know where all the bodies are buried," I joked and smiled. For a moment I think I saw fear in her eyes.

"I wouldn't know about any bodies. I haven't been here that long."

"I'm sure you wouldn't." This one was adept at changing the subject.

"There's a wood stove on the old patio," she informed me.

Yes, of course. On the opposite side of the wall. I noticed it earlier.

"Some evenings it's put to good use into the early morning. Do you have plans for later?"

The invitation caught me off guard. It's more dancing, I suspect, but now I knew I would see her again. Rachael stood beside me, close. I got up from the bar and brushed against her, intending to move past. I lingered for a moment, smiling down at her, our bodies touching. It pleased me when she didn't step back. It must have pleased her, too, because she was still smiling.

I've got her now, and I knew it. "I think I'd like to share a warm fire. I'll see you later."

On the way to my room, I detoured,

wanting to check out the stove. It's old, probably as old as the buildings surrounding it. It must get plenty of use, too, for the block wall behind is covered in soot.

There is no firewood nearby.

The restaurant's closing time can't come soon enough, for already I'm anxious. Nervous. On edge. Trying to anticipate what the night will bring. I stretched out on the bed. Thoughts of the swimmer crowded my brain until I dozed off, and then I saw her through an orange glow as if through the fireplace in my room.

I woke up late. I revived myself by splashing cold water on my face. Scrambled to find my clothes in the dark. I opened the curtains to let in the moonlight without turning on the lights.

Did I miss out? I might have.

In haste I danced my clothes on, barefoot, on the cold tile floor. I pulled on my boots and stumbled along the path to the darkened restaurant. I arrived in time to see Rachael silhouetted against the dim light glowing behind her.

"I was just coming to get you," she said. Something rattled in her hand.

"I slept for a bit. I'm glad I didn't miss out on the fire." It was a keyring.

"You wouldn't have missed it. I wouldn't let you."

I'll bet she wouldn't.

Someone—Rachael, I suspect—has left out bags of kindling and paper that wasn't there when I passed by earlier.

"Well, now that we're both here, why don't I get things going?"

"Don't light the fire without me." She's insistent, so I crumpled paper onto the grate, then pyramided kindling on top. Rachael returned and I held out my hand.

"I want to light it."

"I'll find something for us to sit on."

By the time I returned with chairs and more logs for reinforcement, Rachael had the fire blazing. The heat built fast. The wood popped and crackled and jumped. The top of the stove glowed orange and then red. To escape the heat we pushed back from the blaze.

That was the excuse I needed to turn my chair toward hers. "You made a great fire. You must do this all the time."

"Not really," she said. "It's only the third or fourth time since I've been here. Usually someone else builds the fire. I only get to watch. I'm glad you waited."

"It was no trouble." Indeed. Perhaps she is forgetful of our dance by the pool. She looked at me. Orange firelight filled her eyes. It danced on her hair and face.

"Why did you come here?" The question came all of a sudden.

I rambled on about wanting to escape from everything back home. My voice died when Rachael's fingers catch in the glow as she pushed her long hair behind her ears. It's the same motion she used in the pool.

"How long have you worked here?"

She ignored the question. "A cousin owns the place. I do reservations and menus and sometimes help in the kitchen. I pretty much get to do whatever I want. My grandmother lives here, too. I take care of her when I'm not working in the office."

"It sounds to me like you have the perfect job," I told her.

"I'm bored to death most of the time."

Thus the reason for the dancing she did in the pool, no doubt.

The wind picked up and the twin palms standing at the end of the patio started to sway and dance in unison. Old and thick, their brittle, heavy skirts intertwined near the top. They moved back and forth like slow-dance partners locked in an embrace.

"Listen. Can you hear the rustling?"

"They're whispering, but I don't know what they whisper."

The fire cooled rapidly. The popping and cracking of only a few minutes ago is finished.

"Should we put more wood on?" I ask.

"No, it's late. I should go soon."

"All right, but we should stay until it dies."

"Yes," she agrees.

She took a stick and poked at the glowing embers. Somehow, Rachael managed to get charcoal on her temple. I brought my hand up and let it linger, gently massaging the spot. I know how to dance, too. She doesn't flinch but instead takes my hand and turns to look at me.

"I have to go now," she said.

"Now I know what the palms are whispering."

"What's that?" Her question came much too quickly.

"They whisper how much I enjoyed your company," I tell her.

Rachael turned and walked toward the house at the front of the property. When she disappeared into the darkness, I closed up the fireplace doors.

In the dark and alone, I found my way back to my adobe.

Part 2

The root system of the fan palm is comprised of thousands of pencil-thin rootlets, usually no more than fifteen feet in length. This mass is so thick and dense that competing vegetation rarely penetrates the space occupied by the root system.

Taking Root

It was mid-morning by the time I was awake. I splashed a little water around and felt good enough to wander down to the patio. I made my way past last night's stove and pick a table in the sunny shelter of early morning warmth and settle in. Almost immediately I'm rewarded. Rachael walked past, and I invited her to sit and join me. She can stay for only a minute.

I lingered for most of the morning like that, pleased each time Rachael passed by. It reminded me of the dance in the pool, and I think she is dancing again.

On purpose, again.

"Okay, I can stay for a while now," she admits before sitting down. "I'm on my break."

Finally.

"Well then, let's have lunch," I offered.

"Sit at the bar. I'll be right back," she replied.

She returned with bowls of soup and a bread basket and sat on the corner of the bar to face me. Our feet mingled and she trapped one of mine between hers.

"I made the soup today. Do you like it?"

"I didn't know California women could cook. I thought you all hung out in a valley somewhere and went to malls."

She gave me a half-hearted kick under the bar.

"I know, I know." I laughed and held up my hands in mock surrender.

"Tonight I'm walking into town for dinner. It's not because of your cooking, either. When you're done for the day, why don't we go together? I know I'd enjoy your company and it'll get you out of here for a bit. How about it?"

"Give me a chance to make some arrangements and I'll let you know," she told me.

There's no doubt in my mind. She will be there.

I spent the afternoon wandering around a town that stretched out along the highway in that typical small-town way. Everything fronted on the main street, the very same highway that passed through town. It was as though anything away from the main drag would wither and die. And perhaps it would in this part of the world. There was little to serve anyone passing through. A restaurant or two. Gas stations. A couple of old motels in dire need of repair.

Cars and trucks raced along the main road in a hurry to get somewhere else. An absence of traffic lights ensured nothing would slow down or stop. There was nothing to halt the daily exodus to bigger and brighter places not so far away. Perhaps that's why the town appeared so desolate and looked to be dying.

Finally, I gave up and headed back as fast as I could to where I knew opportunity waited. I was on edge, knowing I'll see Rachael later tonight.

I wondered about the dancing we would do.

Rachael met me at the bar, and it was time for the slow dance to begin. I'm confident I already knew how the night was going to end. I hoped she was of the same mind.

"At last we have some time alone. I was thinking it would never happen." This after we made good our escape from the place.

"Do you do this often?" I wanted to know. If she did, I was sure she wouldn't say.

"Go out with guests? No, I don't. I wanted to get away for a while and forget everything about this place."

"In that case, I'm glad you're doing it with me," I told her.

"I am too. I enjoy your company."

My questions came easy. "If you weren't stuck here, what would you be doing?"

So do her answers. "I'd like to spend a summer in Montana on a ranch to see what that would be like."

"Montana has some nice country. I've ridden through some of the best parts of it."

"One day I'd like to own a bed and breakfast. Not too big. Maybe only for six or so."

"It sounds to me as though you know what you want."

"Yes, I do. If I set my mind to it, I'll get it, too. I always do."

The restaurant was on the edge of town, set back from the road. The interior was covered in bright red—walls, floor, seats, tables. One look had us grinning back and forth until we got set up in a booth. The server left us red plastic menus on the table.

"I'm from a land known for its taco hell."

Rachael smiled. "Taco hell? I'm not familiar with that particular brand of hell."

"I don't know a thing about Mexican food. In any case my eyes haven't adjusted to this place yet."

She smiled again. "Don't worry. I'll order for you if you like."

"How about explaining some of it to me so

we can work on it together?" I asked.

She slid closer and her hand lingered over mine on the menu. A thigh pressed. I pressed back, gently. She moved away, but only for a second, and then her thigh is back, pressing hard against mine. I didn't allow it to escape a second time.

Eyes met, looked away, and met again. The meal was only a backdrop for what is going on between us. I lowered a hand to her thigh. She didn't flinch. Didn't pull away. She moved her leg up to meet my hand and covered my hand with hers. I left it to rest against her. There was heat in both of us. She moved closer. Ever so slightly she began squirming against me as my hand continued stroking her thigh under the table.

Finally, I had enough.

"We need to get out of here."

"Yes." Breathless.

We closed ranks on the return, advancing shoulder to shoulder against the cool desert night. Finally I put my arm around her waist and pulled her to me. "Do you mind?"

"Not if you don't."

She did the same.

"Can we switch to the cold side later?"

"Yes," she laughed.

"In that case I'm glad it's not warmer."

"Me too."

We grinned back and forth. Our pace slowed now that we were dancing in step. On the grounds of the motel peals of laughter erupted from where we spent last night by the fire. Guitar sounds are interrupted by more laughter. We stopped and peeked over the wall.

"Someone stole our fireplace. We're going to yours," Rachael announced.

She's direct. I liked that, but it's not surprising after the dance we did all through dinner. "We're going to need wood. There's none in my adobe."

"The woodpile is over here." In the pitch black she took my hand to lead the way. We stumbled. Laughed. Bumped against each other. Searched for kindling and logs in the dark. Finally we came up with two arm-loads.

"This will last into next week."

Her response is quick. "That's the general idea, isn't it?"

That depends.

We fumbled our way in the dark to my adobe. Together we crashed past the gate and through the door. Firewood tumbled onto the floor. Rachael crumpled paper and puts kindling in the hearth while I locate matches.

"Would you like to do the honors again?" I asked. I knew the answer already.

"If you'll let me, yes."

She kneeled to light the fire and then turned

out the light. I sat on the floor with my back against my bed. She sat down between my spread legs. Her back leaned into me. In the orange darkness my hand searched out hers. Our fingers joined. We stayed like that, silent, listening to the crackling fire.

I raised my hand to caress her face. She turned toward me and our lips met, tentative at first. Warm. Tasting. I cupped a breast. My fingers brushed a nipple. Already it is thick and hard. Her breath quickened.

Suddenly Rachael moved with a start and checked her watch. "I have to go right now."

I kissed her again before I allowed her to get up. "Come back when you can. I'll leave the door open for you."

She stood up and made for the door. "I'll try not to be too late," she said.

Is it a promise?

The fire started to die. I gave up and undress before climbing into bed.

Hinges creaked just loud enough to disturb my sleep. The door closed. Someone was in my room. A shadow revealed itself in the light of the almost-full moon shining through the window.

I'm instantly on alert, but suddenly I found myself admiring Rachael's silhouette. She slipped her nightgown from her shoulders. It dropped to the floor in front of the fireplace. She was naked beneath, and I silently approved of the shadow her breasts and hips display in the dim light.

She brushed hair away from her face and tucked it behind her ears. Finally she leaned down and lifted the covers. Her long, slender body, cooled by the night air, soon warmed as she stretched against the length of me.

"This is a surprise." Not really. But it was pleasant all the same.

"I wanted it to be." She reached to search for me under the sheets and sighs when she finds me. "Oh. What's this?"

Rachael stroked the half-hard length of me and then her cool hand moved farther down. She lingered, fingers fondling first one, then the other, finally getting both in the palm of her hand. She whispered. "They're huge. And heavy. I can feel the heat in them."

Her breathing turned ragged as she moved both hands to cup and pull at me in a milking motion. "The heat."

"That's what you get when you let a man watch you undress when you think he's sleeping. I'm going to throw another log on the fire, all the better to see you with."

I pretended to roll over her to get out of bed and when I did her hands grabbed for me, trying to pull me back down.

"Warm me up with what I had in my hand." Her voice was suddenly hard and edgy.

"I'm not going far," I told her.

"No. You're not."

I got up and she swung her feet to the floor and sat on the edge of the bed, naked, leaning back on her elbows. Waiting. Impatient. I turned to face her.

"Now get over here," she commanded. Hands grabbed for me and her mouth was on me in an instant. She sat and sucked, greedy, devouring. She stroked and pulled with both hands until I'm hard for her. Satisfied, she rolled onto her back. Her feet were off the bed. Her knees were spread wide. Welcoming.

Rachael's voice was commanding. Her hands grabbed at me and her mouth is on me in an instant. She sat and sucked at me, greedy, devouring. She stroked and pulled with both hands until I'm hard again, and then she rolled onto her back. Her feet were off the bed. Her knees were spread wide. Welcoming.

"So soon?" I asked.

"Yes."

I moved and over her she wrapped a hand around me and pulled me hard against her wet opening. Both hands snaked to my hips as she tried to force me into her. "Give it to me all at once."

Now I knew what she liked.

She pushed her hips off the bed to meet me and I plunged into her as deep as I could go in one solid thrust. She cried out. Grunted. Allowed her hips to drop back to the bed.

"I can't move. Hold still."

"I thought you wanted it all at once, woman."

"I do. I like it like that. But you're thick for me," she admitted. More grunts and then she began to moan. "It's the size of you."

"But you had to try, didn't you?" I start to move on her.

"Oh. Yes. Like that. Oh. Go easy for a bit. Hold still. Easy. Easy."

She reached around to get at me, squeezing and fondling, from one to the other and back. She managed to get both in her hand and hangs onto them. I feel her lifting, feeling the weight.

"They're so heavy. The heat in them. They're sweating. Your balls are sweating. I can't believe they can be so hot like that."

"It's all your doing, woman."

"No. I'm almost there. Don't move. Let me hold them. Oh. Oh. I'm coming. I'm coming." All the while she cupped and pulled at me in a steady rhythm.

I felt her open for me. The wet ran out. Her slow hip-rocking against me helped me fill her. When she finally had all of me she wrapped her legs and locked her ankles over my back.

"You've got all of me now," I told her. I began moving with her. There was more grunting.

"Yes. Oh. Damn. I can feel the heat of you against me. No more easy. Hard now. Go hard. I can take it. Leave some of that heat in me,"

Rachael pleaded

I started to move and her grunting stopped and she started moaning again.

"I'm full of you. I can't take any more," she panted. But she does.

Rachael is giving me the ride of my life.

The warmth of the sun beamed through the window woke me. I pulled down the covers to get a better look at what I couldn't see in the dark last night. There's definitely a body under those sheets. I don't pull the covers back up.

Rachael came to with a start. "Oh shit. It's daylight. I have to get out of here."

She bounced out of bed and tried to dance into her nightgown but gave up and sat on the edge of the bed to pull it on. "I'm sore."

She looked at me and smiled as she pulled it up over her breasts in slow motion. First one, then the other disappeared. She was putting on a show just for me.

Through the window I watched her struggle barefoot across sand and gravel and past sagebrush. When her nightgown caught on an errant cholla she tugged at it desperately in her haste to make good her escape.

We met the same way every night.

First, I showed up at the pool to watch

her performance in the subdued late-afternoon light. She wore a bikini now, and her dance has become more reckless. She drops her towel at my chair, and when she has had enough, she climbs out and bends in front of me, teasing and with purpose.

We walk to dinner and then back to a fire in my room. The first time she bends to pull the sheets down, I take her like that and tell her it's the way I want to take her at the pool.

"If there was a way, I'd let you," she admits.

She matched my thrusts by pushing back against me, reaching between her legs to milk me. When I filled her, she turns and sits and takes me in her mouth. It worked. She lies back, and I climbed on again.

Her grunts and groans lasted into the night.

She left at the same time every night. She told me it's to help someone or other get ready for bed—and she returned at the same time, threading her way through the sagebrush behind the adobe.

I adopted the habit of leaving my door unlocked, and each night she performed her ritual. Her greedy mouth and hands went to work on me, and then she's on her back, taking her fill. Her wild, unintelligible outbursts echo through my room, regular and unchanging— music to accompany the dance I eagerly anticipated each night.

Part 3

The fan palm's growth is limited in areas of low water or cold. In shade it grows faster and has a smaller trunk than those growing in full sunlight. New-growth leaves emerge vertically from the growing tip of the trunk, pushing aside the old. If this growth tip is injured—as it can be by fire—the palm tree dies.

Dying Palm

I was restless, and becoming even more restless by the day. While the days were getting warmer and filled with sunshine and blue sky, I'm missing out on good riding weather that would take me farther south. Winter's blast of cold air would arrive soon enough to last until spring.

It wasn't all my fault, though—or was it? I felt free to cast blame on the vixen who haunted my nights with her nocturnal visits. Weakened as I was in my carnal desire for Rachael, I needed to make good an escape from this woman who I was certain wanted to chain me to her fits of midnight madness.

The desires Rachael first ignited in me with her swimming exhibition was gone, chased away by the woman literally sucking the life out of me each and every night. At first, I allowed my body to be taken over by her raw emotion. It pleased me, for what man would turn down hot, sweaty, no-strings sex with a woman such as her?

I realized, finally, that Rachael's crazy desires are something I can never satisfy. The longer I hang around, the more she feels encouraged to indulge herself in her depraved desires. I don't need any more of her. What we shared at the start was taken over by her needs. What was two is now one, hers alone.

I made up my mind. Tonight will be my last. I'm revved up and ready to hit the road. I figured on spending one more night letting Rachael rub herself all over me. Surely it can't be such a bad thing. I even think I'll tell her I'll be leaving in the morning.

In the end, I think not.

I became too complacent about our relationship—or the lack of one. Night after night she hurried back and forth to my room at her convenience, not mine. She no longer knocked, but instead opens the door and barges in, unannounced.

"Where are we going for dinner?" she demanded to know.

Always demanding. It was my fault. Over the past days, I've let her think things have advanced between us. I sense she started to feel as though there is something, some small feeling, some sense of future, for us. I knew better, unconvinced that something like that would advance over the course of only a few days.

"Let's stay here," I said. "We can have an early fire and listen to the palm trees whispering by the pool." The wind was picking up. I was sure it would turn into a dry, dusty desert blow before long.

"They don't whisper," Rachael said with a certain finality. "Palm trees rustle."

We fumbled and stumbled against each other in the dark, finally finding our way back to my adobe. At the gate, I stopped and pulled her toward me. She resisted, and instead, turned away to push past me. I followed her inside.

She won't allow me to light the fire. She pushes me down on the bed. I pretended to fight her off, but that only lasted for a moment. She pulled her dress over her head, exposing her body yet again.

She pushed up, naked and unafraid as always. She gripped me and guided me into her before lowering herself as she always does. Her movement intensifies. Her hips circle. Her breasts keep time.

She finished taking her pleasure and leans forward to look down on me. "You're leaving tomorrow, aren't you?" Breathless, as though she could barely wait to finish before getting it out.

"I have business down in Mexico," I said. "I

told you that."

"Where will you go?" she wanted to know.

"I'll be in Puertecitos for a day or two. When I'm done, I'll stop back here and we can spend more time together."

It's a lie, but she couldn't know. Or perhaps she did. Light from the full moon gleaming through the window revealed a look of disbelief on her face. I've started to feel like a coyote slinking away in the darkness of night and I haven't even left yet. I ease out of bed to light the fire. She appeared to be happy with that.

"Come back here and make love to me before the fire dies."

Make love? It's nothing like that. I shouldn't be doing this, I tell myself. Then moonlight illuminates welcoming arms and open legs and we lost ourselves yet again in our own private fantasies.

One last dance couldn't hurt.

Rachael is gone. The fire has gone out with her. The moon is still throwing down pale light and dark shadow through the window. I got up to lock the door and went back to bed, certain in the knowledge Rachael won't return.

A key slid in the door. It creaked open slowly, and I think I must be dreaming. I rolled over in the darkness. I recognized Rachael. She was standing in the doorway, heisting. Waiting.

For what?

Without a word, she approached the edge of the bed. She's still dressed. Did she want to surprise me? Instead, I let her know I was awake, and the surprise was all hers. "I didn't think you'd be back tonight," I said.

The sound of my voice startled her, and she stepped back. "I wasn't going to, but then I couldn't very well leave things unresolved between us, could I?"

She was upset. Even in the dark I could tell. She began to pace the short distance from the bed to the door, back and forth and back again.

"Unresolved? What's unresolved? I'm leaving tomorrow. It's final." What else could I say?

Rachael's pacing intensified. As the floor runs out between us, she turned without missing a step. Her voice quavered. "I want to come with you." Tears glimmer and slide down her face. "Take me with you," she implored. She halted her pacing by the side of the bed.

It's finally time for her to learn she can't come with me. "Yes, and what about the responsibilities you have here? Your family needs you." I started to think this wasn't going to end well.

"And I need you!" she screamed.

The back of her hand moved up to her face as if to wipe away her tears, but her arm keeps going up and up, over her head. Her hand is clenched. I brace, knowing she's going to take a swing at me. It will all be over in seconds.

She brought up her other hand and clenched both fists together. Suddenly everything started to happen in slow motion.

I decided I don't want to take the punch. I rolled across the bed, trying to dodge the punch I know is coming. A flash of silver missed my shoulder by inches. Something ended up sticking out of the mattress. It's a knife, and it's caught in the springs up to the hilt.

Rachael tried to yank it out for another go. The movement pulled her off balance and I had time to grab her wrists. I held on for dear life. I twisted, edging my body across the bed before I rolled us onto the floor. I came up for air, squeezing both her hands in mine.

I yanked Rachael across the room and forced her into the chair in front of the fireplace. She hunched over, elbows on knees, face in hands, shaking and sobbing. The hilt of the knife is still sticking out of the mattress, and I'm left to wonder if she had a gun stashed somewhere.

I needed to get out of here and back on the road. Fast.

"What was that all about?" I asked. "Did it make you feel any better?" I released a single wrist, and

Rachael swiped at the tears streaming down her face.

"No," she pouted, still shaking.

"Here, put this around you." I handed her the bedspread. The knife wasn't stuck in that. It slipped onto the floor. I made a grab for it and wrapped it around her. Finally calm, I tried to console her as best I could. What else could I do? I wasn't going to call the police just because a woman wanted to stick a knife in me.

Like that's never happened before.

Between breaking into sobs and streaming tears, I kept trying to reassure her everything was going to be all right.

"I want to go home. Will you walk with me?" Finally.

"Yes. Let me get dressed." I kept an eye on her, just in case she might have a gun, but she remained in the chair, exhausted by nerves and the struggle.

Together we walked around the back of the adobe to the house. At the door, she stopped and put her arms around me. "Kiss me." Demanding still.

I did, and then she closed the door behind her.

I figured Rachael to be one step away from the nut-house. I didn't want to be here when she used her key to get into my room, next time while clutching a gun instead of the knife she left behind. I got busy packing up and then loaded the bike as fast as I could. I finished, I took a back trail heading to the main road as quickly and as quietly as I could.

I had places to be and people to see, but mostly, I just wanted to get the hell as far away as I can by sunup.

It's a good feeling being back on the road. It's a relief from a hectic hour spent talking a woman out of sticking a knife in me. Wary as ever, I kept an eye on my mirrors. I was looking for any sign of lights reflecting in the dark. There was nothing for twenty minutes or so, and I figured I'm away, free and clear. Then I noticed headlights in the rearview. It looked like they were gaining.

Did I tell Rachael where I was going? I couldn't remember.

Just in case, I twisted the wick and the lights eventually disappeared in the blackness behind me.

Bad Girls

Lament for another century

The first time I rode through, it was mid-morning, and I was just past the Texas line. I had been riding U.S. 54 all night. It's something I never do any more on that route. Chalk it up to age and knowing better. I was so fatigued I could barely keep my eyes open. I was chilled, too, thanks to riding through the cool night air.

A tired railroad line paralleled the highway. The town had to be an old cow town, as evidenced by the loading pens on the north side of the road. That must have been a long time ago. The wood was turned black by too much sun. The pens were grown over now, forlorn and useless. It looked like they hadn't been used in forever.

I knew by the tired rusted sign hanging over the entrance to Ira's Bar on the opposite side of the highway that it would never be a viable option. Hell, tired as I was, even I could figure out the rusted and broken neon hanging from the wall was long past its best-before date. I recall thinking the place must have had stories to tell at one time, and rode on by.

Just a little farther and I crossed paths with a blue and white café sign sticking up above the flat horizon on a tall metal post. I slowed and pulled off the 54 onto an empty gravel parking lot. I pushed back against a steel hitching post. A motorcycle or a tied-up horse would be safe at the railing in the former cow town.

The building had definitely seen better days, and not recently. The low exterior cement-block walls were painted a dull gray. A low flat roof supported two or three swamp coolers, probably a necessity, given the propensity for the region's hot summers.

Thankfully, I didn't see a window sign advertising the name of the joint as *Mom's*. One of my road rules dictates that I never eat at a place called Mom's. Faded blue and red lettering in the window only said CAFE in huge letters. At the very least, the nameless café would be a safe bet for a bit of grub and a quick coffee to fight the fatigue and cold.

I'd be back on the road in no time. Now that it was daylight, I didn't want to burn any more of it than I had to on my run south.

I entered through the corner door and took a couple of steps down onto a cement floor—thus the reason for the low roof-line. A couple of small tables lined the wall beneath the windows. I headed for the low counter and took up a short chrome stool covered in beat-up, worn-out, thick plastic a couple down from the cash register. If nothing else, I could carry on a little conversation with the woman behind the counter while I drank coffee and warmed my hands.

She poured the coffee into an old-style, over-sized china mug. It glided across the counter and halted in front of me. The mug had one of those thick, rounded handles you could get only one finger in. I nodded my thanks and she raised an eyebrow.

I shook my head and poured in a little sugar from the container in front of me on the counter. While I stirred, I investigated the surroundings, and then turned back to face the woman. She sat in front of the old cash register on the opposite side of the counter.

I took a look at what was inside the pie tray and asked if it was fresh. She said yes, and got up to go into the back. She returned holding a hot metal tray with a dish towel.

That's fresh, I said, and in front of me she sliced a piece and dished it out. Without a word, the woman went back to the kitchen and came out bearing a giant scoop of ice cream.

I grinned, and said thanks, and she smiled and told me I was welcome.

Her smile was friendly. Nothing more.

That broke the ice, and we kibitzed back and

forth, she from her chair behind the counter, and me from the stool in front. I took a better look and figured she was probably in her late twenties or early thirties, with that tired look around the eyes that comes from gaining too much life experience, too young.

Her face was framed by dark hair. Dark brown eyes reflected the light coming in from the windows. I was so stunned that I don't recall checking out the rest of her. I couldn't tear my eyes away from her face.

I did when she started to blush. "Sorry," I said. "I can't help it." Like that was some kind of an excuse. Now I was the one embarrassed.

"That's all right," she replied. "It happens sometimes." She came up with the usual questions. Where was I from? Where was I headed? How long on the road this time?

This time. I noticed that. I volunteered the usual answers, but got stuck on this time.

She noticed that.

I chose to ignore her and instead turned the talking in the direction of some of the places I'd been and the people I'd seen. She not only kept up with me, but managed to get as many laughs from me as I did from her.

I'd call it about even, but not in a Mexican standoff way.

When it came time to go, I really didn't want to, but you know how it goes.

Over the years, I made a habit of stopping by on my way through many times. The cement block walls had been painted many times, and faded just as many. Everything else was the same. So was she. I liked that.

She would be there, sitting behind the counter. She served the coffee, brought me pie and ice cream, and smiled and laughed when the conversation eventually picked up the rhythm from where we left off.

Then I met a girl and settled.

When I unsettled, I discovered the small café closed and locked. Weeds were growing in the expansive parking lot. The café was shuttered permanently against the lonely traveler headed down life's highways. The café and its owner turned into a fading memory.

I missed that place. Even more than that, I missed the friendly recognition and the smiles and the laughter that came along with it.

Chapter 1

Butterfly by Crazy Town. I remember the first time I heard the song. I was on the road, heading north out of Mexico for Nogales. I turned off Mexico 15 for the old Hermosillo-Nogales highway at the cutoff by Aeropuerto

Internacional. I'd crossed there many times.

The semis were always backed up for half a mile or more in advance of *la frontera*. Usually they ended up blocking and filling all the access lanes on the Mexico side heading for U.S. Customs.

I ended up winding my way around the smell of idling diesel exhaust and hot rubber and overheated brakes. That there was never a breeze in the stifling heat didn't help. Most times, the drivers would wave me ahead and slow or come to a halt to make room so I could ride past.

When lane splitting didn't work, I crossed over the wrong way in the southbound lanes and took it from there. The odd time a trucker wouldn't let me in, I gave him the finger on the way by. I made sure never to come to a stop in front of one of those guys.

If you can't imagine why, you don't do much long distance riding.

Off on the west side of the divided highway, the campesinos rested in the shade where they could find it beneath skimpy, stunted trees and shrubs. Manned up and relaxing by their campfires, they were waiting for dark to do what they had to. In a few hours, those same trees would be abandoned and lonely. The campfires would be smoking embers, waiting for the next day's marchers on their way to the promised land.

That would be the last rest they would get until they wormed their way on foot across la línea into the hell of the desert to the north on their way to their destination-if they even knew where that was. Unless they happened across water spotted out by someone sympathetic to their dreams of a better life, it would be a long, thirsty trek, fraught with danger. Sometimes ending in death.

Some would join family members already waiting eagerly. Others, not so fortunate, might be alone and scared while they waited for their ride once they made a successful crossing.

I was always anxious for my own turn in the lineup. Dusty and dry as dirt because my last water was done hours ago. Hungry. Tired. Road weary. Eager to get across. Even more eager to get home.

Nogales. Usually no wind, not even a light breeze if I remembered right. Hot. Stinking exhaust reeking of diesel.

For amusement while I waited my turn in line, I watched the Border Patrol literally heave the illegals back onto the Mexican side faster than I could count. Extradition, U.S.A. style.

Screw 'em if they couldn't take a joke.

When my time came, I pushed back my sunglasses. I wanted to look the border agent straight in the eyes. I liked to let him know I was just happy to be there. Sometimes he'd commiserate with a laugh or a smile or a knowing shake of the head as he waved me through after a perfunctory passport scan.

I crossed at Nogales a bunch of times, and it was always the same. From Nogales it was a 475 mile hop to California and home. Easy. I could do that standing on my head, but always by Valle Verde I'd be looking for cold water and fuel.

Even so, it was still a good day for a ride.

I didn't see her drive in. She must have been there already. I would have noticed a woman in an old Dodge beater that was some color of brown too faded by relentless desert sun. The windows were down. No air conditioning. Maybe it stopped working sometime in the last two decades. If it ever worked. The left front was definitely low.

Maybe she was doing the same thing I was doing. Looking for a little shade and some cold water before heading off to somewhere else. I caught her out looking over my ride parked on the shady side of the building.

Maybe it was the bedroll tied onto the back that drew her attention. If she was smart, she'd notice the back seat occupied by my small duffel. Maybe it would help her figure out I was riding solo. Beyond that, I left it up to her.

Long dark hair. In a ponytail. I liked that. She turned around and I could see it was braided, too. Down to her waist. A nice rear end at the end of it from what I could see. I'd need a better look first, though. I drew closer. She glanced my way. I couldn't see her eyes behind the sunglasses.

She smiled. I nodded and smiled back and pushed my own eyeshades back on my head.

A white shirt with the long sleeves neatly rolled up above her elbows and dark pants and shoes covered off all of her. Too bad. I wondered, though, because even in the plain clothes she looked pretty good.

But then, I was coming out of Mexico after spending the winter.

Maybe she was headed to her shift in a bar. Or maybe a reception of some kind. I didn't ask.

"Would you help me? I can't get my low tire filled and I have to wait tables. I'm going to be late," she said.

It was plain enough. I'd seen her struggle to get the tire aired up. Maybe on purpose. So what, I figured. She wasn't so bad looking. A few freckles here and there, covered with a bit of makeup. Nothing too extravagant.

She handed over the air hose. The movement revealed the inside of her arm. Covered in track marks. Up and back down. Scarred. Old scars. No scabs. Definitely not fresh by any stretch.

"You're all right now," I said. "I can tell."

I don't think she knew I noticed. Her eyes

flicked over me as I finished and stood up.

"I'm definitely all right now. And thank you."

She stood in front of me. Not moving. Like she was checking me out. Maybe her experience working in bars told her I was all right, too.

"It's going to be dark soon. There's plenty of animals on the road at night in these parts," she said.

"It's been a long day in the heat and I'm about wrung out," I said. "I'll take a break, get some water, and carry on."

"You out of Mexico?" she asked.

"Si."

She smiled. "No hablo. Poquito."

"So which is it?" I asked.

"Poquito."

She pushed her own sunglasses onto the top of her head. The movement revealed soft brown eyes. I liked eyes like that. It always made it easy to tell a lot of things about a woman if I could see her eyes. I took another look. I think she did, too.

Her eyes were clear. Her pupils looked to be normal. I already knew mine were bloodshot. Eight hundred miles of wind in a biker's face will do that. The rest of her still looked pretty good, too.

"When did you eat last?" she wanted to know.

The question was plain enough. I must have

looked the sight. I never thought I ever looked hungry, though. "Probably this morning sometime. I've been on the road since before sunrise. Where you off to?"

"I'm working a reception. There's usually a few no-shows. If you want to eat before you head back out on the highway, I could probably arrange it."

"That would be all right. I need a break anyway. It's been a long day for sure."

"You won't be allowed in the kitchen. You'd have to stay out back. You could eat, though, if you wanted. I'd make sure you did."

"As long as there's plenty of water. Give me a minute, okay?" I fetched the key and headed for the men's. I splashed a little water and dried off and minutes later I was good to go.

"I'm Karolina."

"I'm Frank Ross. Pleased to make your acquaintance, Karolina. That's a pretty name."

She ignored that last. Maybe she heard it too often from some and had been disappointed.

"Follow me." Karolina and her beater shook, rattled, and rolled over the curb and out of the gas station lot. I ended up following her to a large banquet hall. She stopped in the huge parking lot out back and popped the trunk. "You can put your things in there."

Maybe I wasn't her first biker after all.

"Walk around the side when you're done. It's in the shade. I'll prop the door open and tell

José to watch for you. If it slows down, sometimes they let us bring out chairs for breaks at the picnic table."

Sure enough, José showed up for his break and I introduced myself. He offered me a smoke. I shook my head and he sat down and lit one. José must have gotten along with Karolina, because he treated me pretty good, too. He brought out water and iced tea and even sat down for another smoke. We chewed the fat, me with my poquito Spanish and he in pretty good English.

"She's been talking about you, *señor*," José said.

"Call me Frank. What's she saying?" I was interested for sure now.

"Only that you helped her get here on time. Her boss doesn't like it when she's late."

"Is Karolina late a lot?" I wanted to know.

"Not since she dumped *el diablo*."

Now I was paying attention. It seemed the two were better friends than I first thought. "El diablo?"

"Her boyfriend," José told me.

Thanks to a customer who never showed for the banquet, I dug into a plate of chicken fricassee. I dug in like a man who hadn't seen food in a week. My table manners went out the window and I was glad there was no one watching. Then José popped out to see how I was doing, and I was forced to slow down.

I gulped water to wash it down and thanked him again. Karolina had to be playing at hard to get. She still hadn't stuck her head out the door.

Karolina's twin in the form of a beater the same faded color as hers, screeched into the dimly lit lot. He made it on four wheels only because the driver was smart enough to stomp on the brakes and slow down. Metal squealed until he let up on the brakes and got out. The door was just loud enough to wake the dead.

And maybe wake the devil, too, according to José. "El diablo, señor Frank."

"Gracias for the warning, José. De nada. It's nothing."

"*Que?*"

José hurried inside, probably to warn Karolina. He was too late. Instead of looking forward to digging into the fricassee for the second time, I was confronted by el diablo screaming Karolina's name from halfway across the parking lot.

I set down my fork and pushed back from the table. I stood up and stepped in front of the screamer as he was about to reach for the door. "You probably shouldn't do that. The person you're looking for is working. You don't want to get her in trouble, do you?"

"Up yours, asshole," el diablo insisted.

"The asshole's name is Frank. Pleased to

meet you, too." I stuck out my hand and made like I wanted to shake his. The confused look was just what I hoped for. I swung a roundhouse into his gut that put him in stop mode.

Diablo backed up a foot or two and put up his fists, thinking it was going to be a boxing match. Then the fancy footwork began and I wasn't about taking chances.

Just in case, I let fly with a foot between his legs. The dancing stopped. He dropped to his knees like a rock and kept on going until he lay doubled up on the asphalt. Both hands grabbed at his crotch. Red-faced and huffing and puffing, it was all he could do to groan and stutter.

"Now be nice, dipshit. When José comes out, I'll send him for Karolina."

I dragged my new friend over to the table. I put a foot on his head, fished for the automatic peeking out of the back of his pants, and tucked it into my own. That should have told me something right there.

Trouble is I only wanted to finish the fricassee. It was tasting pretty good to a man who last had breakfast on the road just past sunrise.

Karolina must have known better than to come out and spend time with me while her ex was still hanging around. She halted at the doorway, looking all concerned. I grinned and winked like I was seeing her for the first time.

"What's for dessert?

She didn't hesitate for even an instant. "If you get rid of that piece of shit stuck to your boot, you can have just about anything you want."

At the beginning of the day, my plan was to ride north to Phoenix to touch base with an old lawyer friend. We went back a long way. I still owed her a pile of dough, though. Isabella would have to wait. I was pretty sure she wouldn't be brokenhearted about it, mostly because she didn't know I was going to look her up.

Chapter 2

Karolina's boyfriend was beginning to get antsy. It could have been my boot on his neck. I removed my foot and let him struggle to sit up. Together with José we helped him stand and eased him in the general direction of his car. I waited for José to depart in a hurry.

"You might want to think about ruining a woman's chances at her job. You don't look to have a whole hell of a lot to offer her if she loses it."

I pushed him behind the wheels and

slammed the door. He put pedal to metal and raced out of the lot the same way he arrived. A few minutes later, I caught Karolina peeking out the banquet hall's open door. With her ex run off, she joined me out back on her break. She brought cake and ice cream and half a plate of chicken for herself.

"Thanks for that," she said. "I'd be getting fired if it wasn't for you."

"Thank José. He's the one warned me. I couldn't have you getting fired before I got a chance at dessert, now, could I?"

Karolina peeled off a spoonful of ice cream from my plate for herself. She put spoon to tongue and worried at it for a bit until it melted and I think I could almost see the wheels turning.

"I've got a place out in Sahuarita. It's not very big. There's plenty of hot water and there's a small spare room," she said.

I waited her out, and she went on.

"You know. If you need a place. For a bit. Temporarily."

Yeah. And if Karolina needed someone to punch out her boyfriend later, that would be me. I wondered how many handguns he could put his hands on.

"Is that your way of telling me I need a shower?"

She smiled.

"Well, according to you, you've been on the

road all day." She smiled across the table again. "You kind of have that scent of dust and sunshine and asphalt about you."

Result. A woman who recognized it for what it was. "You ever have a biker boyfriend?"

"My dad. He rode."

"Ah. A good man. Maybe the three of us can go for a ride sometime," I said. Which was about as much of a promise as I'd ever make in this lifetime.

"He died when I was little. I remember the smell, though. When he came home from a ride he used to pick me up in his arms and hug me."

"I'm sorry, Karolina."

"It was a long time ago," she said.

She wasn't so sad. She had to be over it by now.

"We'll be done in another hour or so. You going to hang around, Frank?" she wanted to know.

"I could." Like I'd be leaving before the second course.

"Then I'll see you after cleanup."

I waited patiently, mostly because I used my jacket for a pillow on the picnic table beside the building. I must have caught at least a couple of hours by the time Karolina and José came out and let the door close behind them.

Karolina greeted me at the table t make sure I was awake before she made off for her junker parked beneath the lot's single light pole. I kept an eye on her just because she was long-legged and walked with a certain gait special to all the girls I ever knew.

Her junker wouldn't start. The engine turned over one time and then the starter began its clicking sound. No one could come up with cables so she threw a leg over and climbed on the empty seat like a pro. She settled back and hung on tight. Her thighs squeezed and her arms went around snug.

Not so tight that I was about complaining. That I ever would.

Karolina leaned into me. Her lips moved against my ear, giving directions while making wordless promises. I wondered if she'd keep them while she gave directions to north of town.

The trailer was old. Not so big. My single headlight played over the side and I could tell it was sunburned and bleached out just like her car. She waited for my signal. I steadied my ride before she eased off. I dropped the kickstand and joined her on the hardpack desert sand and gravel.

Karolina walked up three steps and opened the door. She reached in and flipped a switch and the inside lit up, revealing neat and tidy. Everything had a place. Dishes were put away. No piles of papers and unpaid bills littering the counter or the table. No laundry stacked and drying in piles or thrown over furniture. She wandered down the short hallway turning on lights.

"The bathroom is down here. I'll put out a towel for you. You go first and then I'll have mine."

"Why don't you go ahead. It's your shower. You've been on your feet all day. I've been sitting down."

"All right then. One more thing, though." Karolina hesitated.

Here come the rules, I figured.

"The handgun tucked into your belt. You planning on doing anything with it? Like rob a bank? Or a drugstore?"

I raised my eyebrows. To be honest, I'd forgotten all about it.

"Yeah. I wondered what was digging into me in all the right places and making me happy, so I pulled up the back of your shirt and checked." She grinned and I thought maybe.

"That belonged to your boyfriend," I told her. "I took it away from him before he could hurt himself." That was my story. I might stick to it. I might not.

"It figures. He never did get the gift of brains god gave to most other men. And he's my ex boyfriend. Just so you know."

"He didn't get the message, did he?"

"Nope. Not so far."

I slipped the magazine and checked the action. One in the chamber popped onto the table. "He was prepared, I'll give him that. Does he chase after you often?"

"Not so much any more. I would have lost my job if he made it into the hall tonight, though. Old people don't like seeing stuff like that." Karolina headed off to the shower. She exited in a shorty robe and a towel wrapped around her hair. No pretense there.

It was my turn and I didn't take long before I changed into clean jeans and a fresh shirt. I felt good after breathing asphalt and road dust all day in the heat.

"You clean up not too bad, stranger." Karolina took her long legs and her shorty robe down the hall. She returned looking good in shorts and an off-white blouse. It set her pale skin to glowing. Like most women, I think she knew it, too.

"You don't look so bad, either," I told her.

"Thanks. You want to sit outside and help me count the stars?" Karolina didn't wait for an answer. She opened the fridge and pulled out two bottles and led me out back. Judging by the setup, I figured she did that a lot. Chairs and a table and a *chiminea,* an outdoor fireplace, sat forlorn and alone.

She pulled her chair beside mine and handed me a beer with just enough sweat on it to make it feel good when I swallowed.

"You mind if I run my ride back here? If your ex gets to driving by and doesn't see the car, maybe he'll think you aren't home."

She followed me around the front. I untied my bag and held it out for her.

"If you're looking for it, it's in my bedroom," she said as she took it inside.

She looked good walking away in those shorts. Long, shapely legs climbed the steps. I waited until the door closed before I pushed my ride around back. I didn't wait for Karolina to show up.

My bag wasn't the only thing I found in Karolina's room. She was sitting up in bed, reading. A single faint light illuminated just enough to encourage me to keep going. Long, dark hair tumbled over bare shoulders and fanned across the white pillow as backrest.

Karolina leaned over, placed the book on the night table, and pulled the covers aside.

"You were asking about dessert a while ago. You should probably turn on the air conditioner before you dig in."

I turned on the air conditioner.

The a.c. rattling in the window was doing its job too well. I climbed out of bed and switched it off. I left Karolina sleeping peacefully and pulled on my jeans in search of a beer before heading out back to wonder at my good fortune.

It was good fortune, or the devil was playing

his usual game with me.

Soft footsteps crunched on the hardpack behind me, approaching slowly. Karolina. She probably thought I'd crawled off in the night like a coyote.

"I'm still here," I announced. "Look at how bright those stars are."

The empty chair scraped across the gravel and I pulled it closer.

"You'll need a blanket. It's cooled off a lot."

My chair tipped sideways. I saw more stars close up before I collapsed on the sand. I was freezing cold on the ground by the time I came around. I staggered into the trailer. The bedroom was empty and Karolina was gone. I didn't need a note to tell me her jealous ex was the responsible party.

I started in the small kitchen and came up with a list of numbers taped to the fridge. José's was near the top. I finished dressing and was about to make the call when the door opened and Karolina walked in.

"Where the hell have you been? What happened? Where did you go? I thought your ex had taken you," I told her.

"When I woke up you were gone. I didn't see your bike. I forgot you moved it. I put on some clothes and walked over to José's place. They're friends of mine. I thought-"

So we were both still here. That was a plus.

"I got up and went outside to look at the

stars. I thought you woke up and were coming out to join me. That's when I got a rap on the side of the head that laid me out like cold meat in a reefer. I thought-"

"You thought. I thought. It's cold out here. Let's go back to bed and talk about it while we warm up."

Karolina shook me awake. I checked the clock. The numbers were holding steady at 0530. She flipped on a light and I squinted at the dark window, then back at her. My eyes wandered and stopped squinting at the same time.

"Can't a man recharge for a bit longer? Yesterday was a long one for me, in more ways than one."

"No, silly. I have to go to work," Karolina said. "If you play your cards right, I might even cook breakfast."

An image of this woman dancing naked in front of a frying pan full of bacon took over and I climbed out of bed to dress. I turned in time to get a glimpse of a fine, silk-covered ass being ruined by a loose white skirt. A white blouse covered up the rest of her that the bra didn't.

"I thought you were going to make breakfast." Disappointed, I almost crawled back into bed but for remembering that Karolina's car was broke down at the hall where we left it.

"Right. I'll start the bike."

Karolina hiked up her skirt to climb on the back, revealing the finest pair I'd seen in a while on a *gringa*. The *Mexicanas* weren't so bad either, though. Except this one was climbing on the back of my bike, and I'd just left her all too warm bed. In my book that made her *número una*.

She put lips to my ear, like she did last night. "You didn't get to look last night. The lights were out. Disappointed?"

"The only thing disappointing me this morning is that I had to leave your lovely, warm body and bed and take you to work."

"You can come back after you drop me off." Her lips repeated last night's motions against my ear. This time, they took me to the small diner where she worked. She made sure to give me another show of gorgeous thigh when she climbed off.

"You coming in?"

To say Karolina looked disappointed when I told her I had things to do would be an understatement. I think she must have thought I'd be collecting my things before heading on down the road. Except I wasn't.

I recognized José through the diner window and waved before riding off to the banquet hall and the woman's car. I raised the hood. A quick look at the mess of a battery and I went off to retrieve a cheap version. I popped it in, fired up, and Karolina's car was good to go.

Back at the diner, I let José know the car had been fixed. I settled in at the counter to be waited on by one of the most beautiful woman I ever had the pleasure of looking at. In my absence, Karolina had put on just a bit of makeup. She left off the lipstick and instead had put on only a little lip gloss. At least, that's the way it looked to me.

"What're you having, biker boy?" she asked, as she sidled up to me.

"Can I have more of what I had last night?"

José appeared out of the kitchen, grinning. "No, señor. We don't serve fricassee."

Karolina blushed a bright pink. José and I laughed and laughed some more. The customers didn't know what the hell was going on, which was probably a good thing.

"José, if you know what's good for you, you'll get back in the kitchen or I'll tell your wife," Karolina threatened.

I slapped hands with José and he disappeared.

"Frank, you're getting eggs easy, sausage, and hash with a tomato side. Like it or lump it," she told me.

"Great. Can I have dessert later?"

Karolina didn't miss a beat. "Pie with a side?"

"I fixed your car. It was the battery. I replaced it." I handed over the keys and wondered what kind of dessert that would get me.

"In that case, I get off at three. You can have dessert at my place."

Karolina bent a finger and motioned for me to move closer. I leaned over the counter. She bent, put her lips to my ear, and whispered. "The only thing on the menu will be me. And I won't be on my side."

It was my turn to blush like a schoolboy. I caught José grinning at me from the other side of the pass-thru.

I waited out Karolina's shift at the diner. When it ended, I pushed the empty coffee cup across the counter. Together, we headed outside to my ride. She hung on tight and I think she must have had a grin pasted on her face all the way to the banquet hall at the prospect of picking up her car. I knew, because I kept checking out her reflection in the mirror.

The smell was something else. By the time I got to the empty lot, the stench of burned rubber and gasoline fumes was overwhelming. I knew it wouldn't be good. I was right, too, when we rounded the building and the smaller worker parking lot in back.

Karolina's car was a smoking, burned-out, empty hulk of metal reeking of gasoline and the stink of burned rubber.

"Damn, Frank. I can't afford another one. That son of a bitch-"

"You think it was your boyfriend?" I got off the bike and took a better look. Broken glass was scattered beneath the gas tank. By the look of it, it was a Molotov cocktail that did the job. "Yeah, I think you're right. What do you want to do?"

"What I want to do is go pick up that gun you left at my place and teach the son of a bitch a lesson."

"Well, I can't have you ending up in jail. I'd have to bring you dessert, and believe me, it's not the kind of dessert we've been serving each other so far."

"I know, Frank, but damn it-" She stomped her foot in frustration, hiked up her skirt, and climbed onto the back of the bike. "Let's go home."

I waited for Karolina to get out of her work outfit. She changed into a pair of blue jeans and a shirt. I held out the helmet I found in a closet. "You want to go for a ride?"

"You're making me wear one? Where's yours?" she asked.

"All right. You win, stranger." I pulled my old helmet out of the trunk and put it on. "Let's ride."

Karolina climbed on the back like the pro I knew she was.

I hesitated before punching the starter. "You need to show me where your ex lives, girl."

"You're not gonna do something stupid, are you?"

"Not unless I get caught, baby."

The boyfriend's yard was filled with an RV and a couple of boats. Two new trucks sat in the driveway. A brand-new car squatted on the curb. Which begged the question: why was he driving a wreck when he chased Karolina down at the banquet hall?

"You want a car or a truck?" I asked, only half serious. Her comeback was quick.

"The car, please. I'm not a truck girl. And just how do you plan on putting your hands on that car? I don't want to be driving something that's stolen."

"How is he funding all of it?"

"Drugs, most likely," she said. "Or illegals. All the while I went with him I never knew him to have a job."

"Yet you worked every day."

"Yep. That I did. I can't be sitting around all the time. And I won't be having any kids to keep me in jail at home. Just so you know in advance."

Yeah, there wouldn't be much chance of that happening. At least, not right away. "You need to tell me everything you know about the ex. The sooner, the better if you want that car. I want to know why he drove a beater out to the banquet hall with all those new vehicles parked on his property."

I took Karolina home and she called José. We ended up invited for supper. Showered and shaved and fresh out of bed, we walked to José's place. We took our time, arm in arm, hips bumping hips. It wasn't far, but it took us forever.

"You want to go back to bed?"

"Yes." There was no hesitation.

I halted.

"We can't. José is expecting us any minute."

Karolina knocked and a short woman answered the door. Two little kids hovered at her waist as I was led in by mom and Karolina, who introduced Lupita.

"They'll soon stop being so interested and give you some space."

"It's all right. I don't mind."

I shook hands with José and Lupita gave me a hug. "Karolina likes you-"

"Lupita. Don't tell him that. He'll never leave." Lupita cluck-clucked.

José and I exchanged glances. "Don't worry, Frank. She told me the same thing at the diner."

"Well, I kind of like her too. Plus she makes a mean dessert." I winked in Karolina's direction. Her face and just about everything else flushed.

"We're having American tonight, Frank. Lupita figured you probably had your fill of

Mexican food all winter and you're ready for some down home cooking."

"Well, that's about half true," I told him. "I can eat my fill of either by now. Whatever Lupita wants to do is fine by me."

What Lupita wanted was for José to put the ribs on the barbecue and finish them. I followed him out to the back and slid the door closed. We settled in with a beer while he lit a cigarette and took a long drag.

"What's the deal with Karolina's ex, José?"

"What do you mean?" he asked as he took another drag and let it out.

"Karolina told me he's never worked a day, yet his yard is full of toys. What's going on? Drugs?"

"Maybe. But mostly I think it is illegals. You saw what it was like when you crossed la frontera, no? There are rumors he promises jobs for money. Once they get across, some are sent to him."

"And you know this for a fact?" I asked. I wanted to be sure.

"I think I can say, si. I have many friends who talk about him that way."

"So then, he's a people smuggler. A coyote."

"Not so much that, maybe. But definitely he takes money and promises jobs. The jobs don't pay so much, or end up paying nothing."

"And they end up working for no pay, nothing. Then he's a thief, too. How long did

Karolina go out with him?"

José looked toward the door, checking for Karolina. "I think for a couple of years. She had lots of money to spend for a while. Then they broke up. I don't know why. She ended up in the trailer you see her in. And with the wreck she drives. They must have had some problems."

I'd seen that already. "Someone torched her car in the banquet hall lot."

José answered too fast. "Si. That sounds like something he would do."

"There was broken glass under the gas tank," I told him.

"Yes. He likes that method. From what I have been told."

Lupita rapped on the glass and yelled out the window. "José. Check the ribs, por favor."

"Best not keep the wife waiting, Frank. Time to eat."

Chapter 3

Flashing blues in the rearview jolted me out my good-fortune reverie. After all, who but a cop could put a damper on a biker's dream of being in the wind and hassle-free? I kept my hands on the handlebars, just like I did every time it happened. There was never any sense tempting fate.

"Get off the bike. Put your hands behind your head."

Here we go. "Which is it, officer?"

"Don't give me backtalk." Obviously a man of few words.

He pulled the trigger on the taser. Twin probes inserted themselves into my back forcing my body to spasm. I ended up on my back on top of my motorcycle. I pissed my pants, rolled onto the ground, and lay still.

"That'll teach you to disobey a command from a police officer." For good measure, he gave me another jolt and I went spastic on the ground. Wonder of wonders, but I managed to keep my mouth shut. Either I woke up on the wrong side of the bed and bumped into a wall, or I was in a bad dream.

It turned out to be neither.

"You're under arrest."

"What's the charge, officer?" I figured I should at least know that.

He zapped me again. When I managed to get my shit together, I asked again. I got zapped once more for my troubles. This dumb shit just didn't get it, and that was fine by me. Maybe I didn't, either.

I struggled into the back seat of the cruiser and settled in nicely to attempt to empty my bladder. There was just enough to wet the seat.

My mouth stayed shut all the way to the cop shop. It wasn't a matter of choice. My teeth were chattering too hard to do anything but breathe. On arrival I was ushered into a cell straightaway.

That was a new one on me. I asked for a phone.

Nada.

I asked for a lawyer.

Ditto.

Three days and three meals later, someone had the smarts to let me out. My bike was waiting for me in front of the station. I turned on the key and discovered a full tank of gas. I checked the trunk and saddlebags. My belongings were loaded. I was good to go.

The voice behind me didn't instill any measure of confidence that I'd get away without taking a beating. "Get out of town and don't come back."

I looked across my bike at the familiar ox wearing a badge and a gun. It was the same one that pulled me over and decided on the spot I was guilty. Of what, I never did find out.

"You think it's going to be that simple? You've been watching too many old westerns, dumbass. You'll be hearing from a lawyer. Any lawyer. Because any one of them—even a local law school loser—will take my case and we'll both end up millionaires. Now go screw yourself, Officer Dumbass."

The stupid son of a bitch hauled out his taser and zapped me again. When I stopped twitching, I was back in jail. Jesus, but it was a new century. Didn't anyone watch the news any more?

Then I thought they were probably too busy drooling, watching cop shows at the chief's house, drinking 3.2 beer, and all of them too stupid to have a thought.

I got out a week later, six meals thinner and only a little smarter. My first phone call was to a lawyer I used to know in Phoenix. I'd been on my way to see Isabella when I got sidetracked by Karolina's flat tire. Isabella told me she'd drive down as soon as she cleared her calendar. In the meantime, she made me promise to keep out of jail.

"You won't be committing any obvious crimes, will you, Frank?" Isabella made sure to ask.

I laughed and told her she knew me better than that. I didn't bother trying to explain what I'd been through. She wouldn't have believed me anyway. "None that will stick after lawyering up with you."

We had a good laugh, but how she did it, I didn't care.

It was close to quitting time when I made my way to the diner. I backed it in and shut down. Karolina's surprised look greeted me as I took a stool at the counter.

"Frank. Where have you been? I thought you left. What's going on?"

The look on Karolina's face went from surprise to shock to amazement as I detailed my experience with the local PD. "You can't be serious. Frank. What the hell?"

"Oh, I'm serious all right. Not only that, but someone went through your trailer and made sure to load all of my belongings onto my bike before handing it back to me when they let me out."

That part got to me. Who and why was a mystery to Karolina, too, until she stated the obvious. "It has to be my ex."

I was beginning to believe her. Was it so far-fetched to take it from smuggling illegals to paying off the police to look the other way? Probably drugs had something to do with it, too. Karolina's ex was proving to be more than just a minor annoyance at having any kind of relationship with the woman.

Karolina promised pie and ice cream. While she delivered, José spotted me a mug of coffee, creamed and sugared just the way I liked it. While José and I waited for the woman to fill us in, she busied herself with clearing dishes and wiping tables.

"Are you ever going to stop and sit and start talking, or do we have to tie you down?" I asked.

And then I started my own wondering. Should I stay, or should I move on? It was what I usually did when things got dicey and I didn't want to play any more.

Isabella would be pissed if I rode off while she was on the way to meet up. She'd be even more pissed if she missed out on the false arrest case she thought I had. I'm sure it was the dollar signs, but even so, I owed her. Big.

"What can you tell me about that ex of yours?" I asked. I washed down the pie by sucking back on the coffee José refilled as we waited more or less patiently for the woman to begin.

"—Randy was the high school football star. Every cheerleader wanted him. I got lucky." She laughed.

"Take a look at yourself in a mirror, woman. He's the one that got more than lucky to have you. Right, José?"

Karolina blushed. "Oh Frank. Stop it and let me finish before quitting time." She looked at the clock. "I've been traveling back and forth with José. Thank goodness he's a neighbor. Anyway. Which reminds me. You have anywhere to stay?" She grinned.

I grinned right back. "Well-"

"At quitting time you can take me home and unpack for the second time. José won't mind in the slightest if I don't catch a ride with him. Right José?"

She never did finish telling me about Randy.

Karolina settled onto the back of the bike like she belonged there for the ride home. We rode to her place the long way. I made sure to pass by her ex's. I cracked the throttle just for spite to let Randy know I was back in town. No one rushed out to wave a fist. And even if he did, I'd have only held up a finger while I rode on by.

I hoped Karolina would be good for me again. She certainly was the first time. I had no reason so suspect otherwise now. I deposited us at the end of her gravel driveway. Just to be sure I hurried in to check the fridge. She'd seen to it that it was stocked, so I dove in.

Karolina devoured my eggs and bacon and toast and I was in like Flynn one more time.

"You're a good cook, too. You're hired. When can you start chipping in on the rent for this dump? My surprise hid behind a smile.

"Any time you want, baby. My stash is in my handlebars. I'll get it for you tonight."

"You won't have time tonight," she insisted. "I have plans."

Karolina dragged me into the shower, and her plans for tonight went out the window by late afternoon. By eight, we were fast asleep. At midnight, we were wide awake. Karolina's elbow was stuck against my ribs and she was banging on my chest with a fist.

The loudest banging was coming from outside. Someone was beating on the side of the tin-clad trailer.

"Good grief, girl. Is there never any peace around here for a tired biker? I just got out of jail, and now it's like I'm right back in with the cops rattling nightsticks against the bars to keep me awake."

"Frank! Frank. Are you in there? Frank?" A woman's voice. And it was loud. I stumbled out of bed and opened the door.

"Put some pants on unless you don't have company."

Behind me, a naked Karolina poked her head out the door. "You can keep your pants on, darlin'. The man has company," she told Isabella.

"Which is why you don't have any pants, if I know Frank. I'm Isabella." She held out her hand and the women shook on it.

"Come right in. We won't be a minute," Karolina told her.

I disappeared with Karolina.

Isabela shouted after us. "Jesus, Frank, do you ever answer a door in your pants?"

Karolina's head shook and she grinned. "I think there must be a story there, but I'm not asking."

That pretty much sealed it. The box of wine

came out of the fridge. Water glasses followed. I left for bed when the cardboard box was only half empty. When I woke up, the two women were cackling like a couple of witches while Isabella pretended she could cook. It looked like the women would be friends for life.

"Sit your ass down, Frank. We have some things to discuss," Isabella ordered.

"Do I have to eat your cooking?"

"Only if you don't want to go back to jail."

Karolina laughed her ass off before heading out the door to catch a ride to work with José. "Try to get along, you two," was her parting shot at both of us.

Isabella retrieved her briefcase, and we commenced getting into it. By the time she finished, I'd signed every piece of paper she put in front of me. I didn't bother reading any of it. To say that I trusted her would be an understatement.

"Frank, I'm telling you now. Unless you die, you're going to clean up. This local PD is a disaster of incompetence and ignorance and just plain stupidity on the part of the chief and all of his relatives on the force."

I must have looked doubtful.

"You're right to look at me like that. It's not going to come any time soon. By the time this works its way through the courts, you just might be an old-timer."

"In that case, I have nothing but time on my

hands. Do I have to stay here?"

"Hell no," Isabella said. "But I think you'd disappoint Karolina if you left too soon. Why not stick around for a while and enjoy yourself?"

Which made only a little sense. Since arriving, I'd spent more time in jail than I had enjoying Karolina. "In that case, I need to know more about someone."

I gave Isabella the name of Karolina's boyfriend and his address and left her to figure out the rest.

"I'll be in a motel for a day or two digging up what I need to know on these clowns," Isabella said. "Stay in touch."

"In that case, join me for a real all-day breakfast feast at the diner. You still can't cook worth shit."

She couldn't, either. I'd been subjected to Isabella's cooking on a number of occasions over the years. We laughed about it now, but I didn't know how to take it at the time. I just ate it and shut up.

"And judging by the way you two look at each other, you're not going to be cooking for me."

"Not on your life."

We were in the process of finishing up. I was looking forward to breakfast at the diner with Isabella in tow. The best part of it all was I'd get the woman to pay, one way or the other. A healthy tip for Karolina wouldn't hurt, either.

Maybe I was counting chickens. Maybe it was my bad luck. I don't know. But when the door flew open and four cops stormed into the trailer, Isabella and I had time for a quick glance before the shit spread pretty evenly between us. It didn't take either of us much to figure out that something wasn't right with the locals.

They forced me to watch as Isabella was handcuffed in the trailer and led out to her Cadillac. The trunk opened and she ended up forced into it. She didn't struggle, wisely I figured. A uniform slammed it shut, got in the driver's side. Tires spun in loose sand, creating a cloud of dust over the rest of us.

It occurred to me that the cloud descending on the local PD was about to be a lot worse than dust if I knew Isabella.

Handcuffed and loaded into the back of a black and white, I wondered if I'd be heading back to jail. Before long, I knew. It was a short, familiar drive. That and the cell was becoming much too familiar.

The volume cranked up on the television in the PD ready room carried into the cells in the small building. Judging by the lack of acknowledgment that they had hit a home run by threatening Isabella, it sounded like they were more than a little dumbfounded.

They were finding out firsthand the abilities of the lawyer I hired to do my bidding. Writs of habeas were handled by her law partner in Phoenix and were presented to a federal judge. It was like she had a premonition of some sort. Of course, the live video feed of our extraction from the trailer coming from her camera'd-up car didn't hurt. That it was recorded onto hard drives back at her office only made the proceedings go a lot smoother.

Even with all of that preparation on Isabella's part and the commotion it caused, I ended up serving another day. This time, there was no meal. Obviously the county was on an economy drive.

The beating I took from a couple of hard-core imposters sent in to share the cell left me wondering when it would end. It was obvious that Randy had more than a single in with the local PD. I left the cop shop wondering if the entire force was related.

There was only one way to find out. I parked on a hill and staked out Randy the ex-boyfriend's place in the rental I picked up. Binoculars and burritos stood in for José's diner cooking and the comforts Karolina had to offer at her trailer.

Randy's nocturnal comings and goings were like clockwork. By the time I had it down, I was more than ready.

I waited until Randy drove off in his fancy new half-ton. I couldn't be certain on the dimly lit street, but it looked like him. He was walking out of the right place. He looked to be the same one storming the banquet hall a few weeks ago.

Satisfied, I took a stroll around back, kicked in the door, and brazenly walked in.

I had no idea what I'd find, but I was in it for the duration. I wandered from room to room, flicking on lights as I went. Searching for something, anything, that might keep Randy off of the police radar. The only thing I came up with was a photo album. A quick look told me everyone in it was family. Everyone in it was on the police force, too. Isabella would have a field day with this information.

I tucked the album under my arm and walked back the way I came in. The lights went out before I managed to flip a switch. When I came to, I was in the middle of nowhere. A huge bonfire lit up the surrounding desert. In the firelight, I spotted the front end of Isabella's Cadillac.

If she was still in the trunk, she had to be a mess by now. Would she still be alive after sitting in the desert heat locked in her trunk? There wasn't a thing I could do. I was busy taking a beating administered by two of the deputies while Randy looked on. The smug look of satisfaction said he didn't have a care in the world.

"Leave him for now," Randy said. "That should be enough to discourage him. "I have to get back to town. There are people arriving that owe me money, and I intend to collect. If I don't get paid, neither will you."

I ended up slammed to the ground. My wrists and ankles stayed handcuffed. If I wanted to walk away, I couldn't do it. I was left alone with Isabella's car. There wasn't anything I could do for her but pop the trunk. She crawled out with an automatic in her hand and a bottle of water with a nice sweat running down the sides. She handed it over while she unlocked the cuffs.

"I was in a similar situation a few years ago," she explained. As if that was good enough, she went around to the trunk for another bottle. She cracked the top and guzzled. "I learned to be prepared for the fool who thinks he's threatening me by keeping me alive. Now get in. We're going back to town."

Those poor townie sons of bitches had no idea the hell they unleashed.

Chapter 4

In **Isabella's absence, raw** CCTV footage of her escapades at the trailer and in the desert had been uploaded to her web site. A computer guru she had access to edited the footage. The guru had to be a wizard. It took some bit of editing to compress and then assemble the elapsed times between the interesting parts.

When it was ready, the final version was forwarded to local television news. All of the stations played the same loop over the dinnertime news hour. Even the radio stations were carrying a version, although somewhat diminished by the lack of a video stream.

Isabella's phone rang non-stop. She answered the questions and filled in the reporters about the ordeal she and her client was put through at the trailer and out in the desert. Of course, all of it was couched in the language of lawyers. I heard the words allegedly and possibly and a few opinions thrown in for good measure.

Through it all, she stayed calm. I don't know how she did it. I was ready to rip heads off, but she knew that wasn't a solution.

"The only thing anyone will understand is a

lawsuit, Frank. Doing what we both want to do would be the worst thing possible. I know that. You should, too, by now. Just look where we are."

Isabella was right, of course. Between us, we managed to experience more cop grief than a black man out for an after-dark walk in a white neighborhood. The question was, how long would it go on before someone put a stop to it?

Isabella took us to the diner where Karolina greeted us with hugs and fresh coffee when we arrived. "I thought you two had eloped until I saw the news. I'm glad you're safe."

Isabella plopped into a booth and cracked her briefcase. "Frank wouldn't do anything like that. He already knows I can't cook worth a damn. And he makes some mighty shitty coffee, too, so we're pretty much even on those scores."

Karolina's eyes moved in my direction. "So that's why you always cooked. No wonder I had to get up to make the coffee. You wouldn't drink your own."

Talk about hitting a sore spot. I held up my hands in surrender while the women grinned. "You know, it's not nice to laugh at someone."

"We weren't laughing at you, Frank. We were laughing with you."

Isabella pushed across another sheaf of papers. I signed like my life depended on it. And maybe it did, but now Karolina had been dragged into it, too. She would need some protection from Randy, her ex.

"Now then, Karolina-" Isabella explained restraining orders and how they worked—or didn't, as the case may be. At the end of it all, Karolina signed without question.

"Let me remind you. It doesn't mean that they'll stay away from your place. If someone breaks the law—she looked at me like I was the criminal—they have every right to pursue whoever it is. And they can still make shit up."

"So what's changed?" I asked.

"They know we're onto them. If they haven't figured it out by now, they're dumber than a box of hammers," Isabella said.

Given the way the local brownshirts were treating us, I figured they were a bit short of more than a few boxes of nails, too.

"I'm headed back to my office. If you two need-"

Karolina interrupted her. "You better text me when you get back to the city. Or else."

She didn't say or else what.

Karolina's shift ended and she hiked up her skirt and climbed on behind me. Being the man that I am, I never got tired of a woman's long, shapely legs. Hers were no exception. We arrived home in time to catch the late news. Karolina's dropping jaw and shaking head only served to make Isabella's video clips all the more absurd. We settled in for the night by drinking coffee and trying to convince one another that our problems were over.

Isabella was a firecracker looking for a place to explode. She'd definitely found one in the form of the local PD. The only thing wrong was that it could explode on us first before Isabella managed to catch up to the dirty cops.

"I'm thinking Randy can't be too happy with what's going on. His little kingdom has been falling apart since I rode into town and got tangled up with you."

"Let's go to bed and talk about it," Karolina said. It wasn't a suggestion.

We abandoned any pretense of talking minutes after tearing off our clothes and kicking away the sheets. The instant the lights went out, more pounding echoed on the tin and into the trailer. It was like someone had been peering into the bedroom window waiting for the fun and games to begin. This time, both of us were forced to endure the absurdity of the local PD's incompetence as they stormed into the trailer.

They permitted us to get dressed before leading us, handcuffed and in chains, into the back of a van. We were unceremoniously tossed inside. The door slammed and we were driven off.

It wasn't the short ride to town I'd become

accustomed to. After going from smooth pavement to bouncing dirt road, the vehicle slowed and then stopped. A rattling gate opened, the van drove past, and then past another gate and we were in a lighted yard. The compound was surrounded by steel fence topped with razor wire. What looked to be structures in a huge prison complex towered over us.

"I guess this is where we say goodbye. How long do you think it will be before Isabella finds us?"

A guard smacked a nightstick against the palm of his hand. "No talking. Eyes straight ahead."

"I don't know, Frank, but I'm thinking she's going to make a pile of money thanks to us," Karolina said. For her trouble, Karolina ended up on the ground. She twitched and screamed as pain twisted her face. She managed to look up at me through slitted eyes.

"See what I mean? Big money. When she doesn't get a response to her text, I'm thinking she'll be right back with the Feds."

Karolina was right, although it took Isabella some bit of time to locate us. She dutifully showed up at the prison and loaded us into her Cadillac. Neither Karolina nor I asked any questions. We were exhausted, mentally and physically, from the week-long ordeal.

On the drive back to town, Isabella filled us in on what she'd been doing since we were imprisoned illegally, among other things on her laundry list of crimes committed against us. It wasn't pretty.

"Things have been happening in the background since my videos went live. The local mayor and council has been removed from office. Everyone on the local PD has been relieved of duty. The state police have replaced them temporarily."

Which was all right by any measure of accountability, but- "So what's a poor boy and girl to do?"

"Well, you can't go back to your place, Karolina. It's been torched." Isabella looked across at me.

"Your bike went up along with it, Frank. Fortunately, after the local fire department refused to respond, a souvenir video surfaced taken by a compadre. It shows one of them tossing a couple of Molotov cocktails through the windows of Karolina's trailer."

When that happened, we were on our way to prison. "Just as well we ended up in prison."

"You both have horseshoes nailed to your asses. Are you having any trouble sitting down with those lumps?" Isabella laughed.

"That can't be true, and you know it, Isabella. You've seen our asses. And I know for sure I don't clank when I sit down. I can't speak for Frank. All I can do is get him to lie down."

Isabella blushed and I smiled and Karolina laughed and then we all laughed at the absurdity of all of it.

It was the only thing left for us to do.

Isabella loaded us into her Cadillac and drove us into Phoenix. She convinced us to allow her to put us up until things quieted down. We were witness to her television appearances where she made out like a bandit. Even some dimwitted television lawyer had her on, not to mention the morning shows.

Our names weren't mentioned once, which was fine by me.

With my bike destroyed in the conflagration at Karolina's trailer, I poured over the papers and the bike shop adverts looking for another 95 bagger. I found one after about a week of looking.

I convinced Isabella to drop us off and I did a test ride with Karolina. The owner followed on another bike. He recognized us as the pair of desperadoes who'd brought down a police department all by our lonesome.

Karolina started right in telling him about Isabella. I stopped her before she got too carried away, explaining that you can never tell these days who's recording and who isn't. "He doesn't need to know about that," I told her.

She quieted down, although she looked disappointed, as though the wind had been let out of her sails.

Satisfied that the bike seemed to be in good mechanical shape, I headed off to a bank with the owner where I dished out the cash. Now all I needed was an address and I'd end up plated in Arizona—which wasn't a problem for Isabella. She had me fixed up in no time.

"We need to find a place of our own, Isabella. Until this all shakes out, we're going to be in demand by just about everyone from the state, the feds, and the rest of the losers back in bumwad, A-Zee."

Karolina nodded in agreement. Isabella looked at us like we were crazy. "Why wouldn't you stay here? It's got a great view. Plenty of security down in the lobby. It's close to trendy downtown. What more could you two want?"

"You're too kind, Isabella, and I'm really grateful. Without you, I'd be stuck in Valle Verde looking for another place. Frank would probably be out of my life, having already put up with enough trouble to last a lifetime."

"I know, but—"

Karolina held up a hand. "You're single. Picture a month of sharing your place with the two of us. You'd end up changing the locks and tossing us into the street just to be rid of us."

Finally, Isabella agreed, and I got the feeling

she knew it to be true. "I know a guy. Let me make some phone calls for you."

Neither of us wanted charity. Isabella located a place out by Chandler. We agreed on a monthly rate for the furnished apartment. It was more than Karolina bargained for. She broke out in tears when I unlocked the door and she got a look at the inside. "I could never afford a place like this, Frank. Never in a million years."

The place was a little much with the modern furniture and the view out the window and the neighborhood, but it was free. Who would say no to that?

"In that case, you better sign up at the local college and find a rich frat boy. In no time you'll be beating them off with a stick."

"At long as I'm not beating them off with my hand-" She grinned before leading me into the bedroom. I was only a little disappointed when she immediately began stripping the bed. She threw the sheets into the washer. "Better safe than sorry. Now let's go for groceries."

"You don't want to eat out?"

"With a place like this begging for two people to share dinner over candlelight? I don't think so, fella."

We loaded the bagger with groceries and headed for home. We hauled our treasures inside, and Karolina set out making what she called a romantic dinner for two. I eased up to the washer, hauled out the sheets, and put them in to dry. While she was in the shower, I made up the huge California king.

With nothing else to do, I headed for the shower.

"Out," she ordered. "I need to get dressed without having you around to distract me."

I hung my head and sheepishly headed for the kitchen. I set the table and waited. And waited. And waited. "Are you alive in there?"

Karolina halted at the door to the bedroom. She hadn't brought much with her, but what she managed to pick up when I was doing the grocery shopping was good enough for me. She was beautiful in a short skirt and sheer blouse. The plain-looking woman with the flat tire I met at the gas pump was almost unrecognizable. "No wonder your friend Randy doesn't want to let you go."

"You already know why, biker boy. You can come back to the bedroom now. I put a hold on the candlelight. Supper won't be for a while."

We took our time. Pillow talk ran out when Karolina suggested we head farther north to get away from her ex. I let her know I'd consider it, but for now we'd be stuck where we were until Isabella didn't need us any more.

"If we're going to go ahead with a lawsuit, we might as well wait it out. We'll have plenty of time to figure out where we're going later."

The woman went all pouty on me. She didn't appear too happy knowing I wouldn't be jumping on the go train just because she wanted me to. It seemed like she got over it after a bit of food and a lot of wine.

Karolina's even breathing told me she was still sleeping. I had to be at a meeting with Isabella first thing. I rummaged through the dresser, searching for anything I had left that was clean. Impatient and in a hurry, I opened one of the drawers Karolina used. It fell out of the track and crashed to the floor. Her underwear scattered at the foot of the dresser. A plastic-wrapped package lay on the floor next to her underwear.

My breath caught. I slid the drawer back in place and scooped up the package. I checked on Karolina. She was still asleep. I deposited the twin packages on the dining room table. The dishes were still in place after we eagerly deserted the kitchen for the bedroom.

It wasn't easy to admit, but at least now I knew why she brought up wanting to head farther north. She had used Randy, her ex, as an excuse. More miles meant more money for the bundles of coca she had stashed with her underwear. I knew all about it from a bad experience a couple of years back.

In the darkened bedroom I quietly packed my belongings and headed for the door. Karolina was still breathing normally. I loaded up and beat a hasty retreat to Isabella's place. Her lights were on. I rang and she buzzed me in.

I wasted no time explaining why I needed to be heading out of town, and fast. I let her in on Karolina's secret. That she was a drug mule had taken me by surprise more than I wanted to admit to anyone—even Isabella.

"Are you sure, Frank? You just want to ride off into the sunset and leave it all behind? You'll get quite a payday when it comes due. I will too, of course."

"I know, Isabella. But I didn't foresee anything like this. I think I need some road time to consider my next step."

She knew I wouldn't be held back. She knew me too well.

"Besides, you have more than enough on your plate with your own abduction and side trip into the desert. You're lucky to be alive."

"I already found a good lawyer friend I trust to represent me. I was hoping it would allow me to dedicate all of my time to your case. You'll end up with enough money to do whatever you want for the rest of your life.

I looked out the window and across the bright city lights stretching out in front of me like a magic carpet. It was way too big for my liking. Too easy to like.

"You know, I'm already doing that," I told her. "I have to count the small change, but it's hassle-free. And I can come and go as I please. When I want. How I want."

I knew she'd have an answer.

"Until it isn't. You already know what that's like. And Karolina shouldn't have any bearing on the treatment you endured by dirty cops, Frank."

"You're right, but all I want to do is get out of town. I'm sure if Karolina needs your help, she'll get in touch. If I were you, I wouldn't hold your breath. She was using both of us."

I said my goodbyes and walked out to my ride. I fired up and headed for a diner I once knew in another life. I took a seat at the counter and ordered the breakfast I would need to put the miles and my troubles in the rearview.

I waited it out, and twilight came soon enough. I paid up and headed out to my ride.

It was a good day to ride.

The desert air was just cool enough for a light jacket and gloves. I slipped on a comfortably faded, worn jacket to keep the cold off that I knew the fresh morning air would bring out on the highway. My tie-downs looked good. There was nothing worse than something falling off that I might need down the road.

I tied my bandana and checked it. I'd be able

to pull it over my lower face in an instant if blowing sand or dust looked like it might interrupt the highway.

I punched the starter and Isabella showed up just as the bike began its throaty idle. "I knew you'd be here. I like the place, too. So long, Frank. I'll keep in touch." She knew I hated goodbyes.

"Thanks for everything. I'll be seeing you."

I reached the city's outskirts in time to witness the early morning sunrise turn the gray, pre-dawn sky into a bright blue. The desert temperature was down. The humidity was up slightly. A biker in the wind would be just about right until high-noon desert heat took over.

I already knew the two-lane asphalt ribbon stretching out in front of me would lead head-on to friends and strangers and an adventure I hadn't yet experienced. If I ended up fortunate, maybe I'd cross paths with a long-haired, tight-bodied hitch-hiker. Or maybe a traveling woman riding her own looking for a little company. A man can't ask for much more than that.

It definitely was a good day to ride.

Road Rules

I've ridden highways and byways across North America and down Mexico way. Sometimes I learned things the easy way. Sometimes I learned the hard way. I found it best to never stop learning, no matter the way.

Never eat at a place called Mom's.

Never ride close to a cage that advertises the driver's name as Sixpack.

Never pull into an isolated, unlit rest stop after dark.

Never walk into a bar where the half-tons in the parking lot have rifle racks mounted in the window—especially if there are rifles hanging off the racks.

If the dancer says she needs a ride home, be generous, but watch your back on the way to the door.

Watch your back in a parking lot.

If you pick up a hitchhiker named Angel on an interstate on-ramp near Deming, beware that she doesn't talk you into taking her to a non-existent music festival on a back road off of Highway 666.

If it feels like it's time to leave, go with your instinct. It's usually right.

When you wake up and find yourself alive and riding on the wrong side of the yellow line, stop and take a break to live a little longer.

And finally, when you wake up and find yourself alive and riding on the wrong side of the yellow line for the second time, stop and take a break.

You'll definitely live a lot longer.

Later Comes Around

I **noticed her right** away, and not because she was the only other person in the room. I liked the look of her long, dark hair neatly piled on top of her head and fastened with a dark comb. The effect emphasized her slender neck and the strong profile of her face.

It was a look that appealed to me.

She was setting tables—napkin, knife, fork, spoon, glass. Something slipped and dropped to the floor—a knife maybe, or a fork—and she mumbled a profanity. Nothing broke, but she dedicated half a glance to the empty room.

She caught me smiling at her. She returned it with one of her own. "I hope you didn't hear that," she said.

"No, I didn't. Would it matter to you if I had?"

"Well, I shouldn't be cursing to myself in front of customers."

"There's only one. I can make the claim I was never here."

"You looked absolutely frozen when you

walked in," she said.

So she noticed, after all. My reward at the end of the long, cold ride south from Death Valley was a mug of coffee at the bar in the old inn's restaurant. I cupped the hot coffee with both hands and hunched over it, hoping the heat would warm my entire body. It was a fruitless effort, of course.

"I'm still trying to get warm. I've been on the road since first light, hoping to outrun the cold weather chasing me. If this is southern California, isn't it supposed to be warm?"

She hedged her response. "Yesterday was warm. Today, not so warm. Would you like more coffee?"

"Yes I would," I told her.

Her dark-brown hair perfectly matched the color of her eyes. I've never seen that before. It must have taken some doing. It couldn't be a coincidence. Even better, without makeup, she wasn't a plain-looking girl.

"Your eyes—" I began.

"Yes, I'm a brown-eyed girl, just like the song."

"You certainly are," I agreed.

Then, just for the hell of it. "I like brown-eyed girls."

"In that case, I'm not so special any more, am I?"

"Oh, I don't know about that."

She smiled. "I like your hat."

I thought she must be one of those women who likes to have the last word, no matter the subject. "It keeps the sun off."

"It's not doing much today, though, is it?"

I had to agree with that considering the dull, sunless day. "I like hats. And brown-eyed girls."

"And this brown-eyed girl likes motorcycles."

That came out of nowhere. "That's a good thing. I'd be disappointed if you told me you didn't." Now I wanted to know how she felt about their riders.

"I'm Frank." I held out my hand. She took it. "Kate."

"The pleasure is all mine, brown-eyed Kate."

I tossed back what remained of my coffee and wandered off to check out my room and turn up the heat. I settled in and rewarded myself by discarding some of the bulky clothes I had been wearing for warmth since the early morning.

The restaurant was mostly empty by the time I showed up for dinner. I was early enough to miss the dinnertime crowd that would arrive later. I took my seat at the bar and convinced Kate to bring me a coffee.

"Are you here to eat?" she asked.

"Yes I am. Where can I sit and keep an eye out?"

She gestured at a table behind me. "How about right there?"

Traffic in the restaurant began picking up. I listened to the gentle buzz of conversation as it increased. After a few minutes, it turned out I wasn't being ignored. A second server showed up with a menu and disappeared. Kate plopped down a bread basket and rushed off.

I've been had, I thought to myself. I've been handed off. No sooner had I thought it than Kate returned with her comments on the soup and the specials.

Tracy took my order. Kate brought it to the table. Tracy wanted to know if everything was okay. Kate refilled my water glass.

"Being waited on by two women is great," I said with a smile. There was no smile in return when that popped out of my mouth. What the hell was I thinking?

"You should be so lucky." Kate was a saucy one, too.

That was the last I saw of her. Tracy brought the bill. I left a tip and paid up at the bar in time to witness Kate clearing my table.

"Are there other places to eat around here?" I asked her.

"Well, I'm a vegetarian, so for me, not so much. There's a place out by the tire shop where you can get pita sandwiches."

That didn't sound promising. I wanted there to be a place where I could offer to take her for a meal, given half a chance. Whether given-half-a-chance would come along for me, I had no idea. What the hell, succeed or flame out. It wouldn't be the first time I attempted the coin-flip.

Instead, I made an executive decision and changed the subject entirely. "You must have long hair if you've got it piled and pinned the way you do."

Kate turned at her waist and drew her hand across her back.

"It used to be down to here but I got it cut a month ago. It's naturally curly. It was too long to manage."

"I like that. When we go for that ride tomorrow, will you wear it up or down?" I asked.

"Maybe neither. I might wear it in a tail."

"That would be all right, too."

"Say, was that an invitation?"

I had her. More likely, she knew she had me. "You're paying attention. And it sounded like you accepted."

"It did, didn't it?"

I stayed where I was and killed time telling lies to the friendly bartender. Nothing new there. Hell, back in my drinking days, all the bartenders I ever knew and some I had forgotten about all proved friendly.

The restaurant crowd finally thinned, and Kate used the quiet time to come over to sit beside me at the bar.

"When I get home tonight, I have to write a paper that's due tomorrow."

I appreciated a woman with an education. I always figured a woman without one was a liability, not an asset. "Well then, I guess a ride after work is out of the question."

"I work tomorrow at four. I could come in early," she said.

"I think you should come in early," I agreed.

Kate didn't come by to say goodbye at quitting time. Instead, she surprised me by parading across the dining room to the door. Okay, so it wasn't parading, exactly, but she made sure I saw her. The thick, dark hair she kept tied up all evening was finally free. Kate rewarded me by letting it cascade over her shoulders and down her back.

At the door, she stopped and turned and caught me looking. I couldn't help it. I smiled and waved, and she didn't seem to mind because she did the same. It was the best I could do.

She pushed through the door and disappeared into the night.

The frigid air that chased after me on my ride south was still hanging around. In the morning, I dressed for a ride into Buena Vista in the cold and drizzle. Later in the day, the sun came through in patches, but it stayed miserable.

I made it back in time to get to the restaurant an hour before Kate's shift began. She was waiting. I took a better look at her in the brown leather jacket and faded jeans.

I'm ready."

"Yes you are. Are you sure you want to freeze your butt off? We could do it later in the week when it's warmer," I volunteered.

"Last night you said tomorrow afternoon. It's tomorrow. It's afternoon. When are we leaving?"

"Impatient, she had her hands on her hips. I couldn't help smiling."

"Well, since you put it that way—but I think we better get some chaps on you and a pair of gloves. I was out earlier and it'll be cold once we get in the wind. Come on, let's get you dressed."

We made small talk on the walk to my adobe. I learned she had recently broken off with her boyfriend of four years. For two of those years, they had been engaged. I didn't fault her in the least. What woman likes long-term engagements?

"But we're still friends. It's just too soon after the breakup to get involved with anyone right now."

"I hear you. For now, you'll be my riding partner," I said.

"I like the sound of that. Wait, what was that? For now?"

I pretended I didn't hear her. "You can leave your bag in my room."

I handed her the chaps, and she struggled to put them on. "Do up the belt first." I helped her wrap them around each leg and pulled the zippers down the side.

"You look pretty good in those chaps. Turn around and give me a better look."

She did, grinning the whole time. "Thanks. I feel good, too. Do I get gloves?"

Then she did it again. This time she halted halfway, and I had a good look at her rear. On purpose, she turned her head and caught me admiring. At the bike, she fumbled with the helmet's buckle.

"Here, let me help with that."

She held up her hands like a surgeon just prepped for an operation, and I pulled thick gloves on for her. She waggled her fingers and gave me a thumbs up.

I hit the starter, and the engine rumbled to life and settled into a steady rhythm.

"Ready?"

"I'm ready. Let's roll," Kate said.

I toed first and eased in some throttle. We shook our way down the rough gravel driveway. When I hit the street, I kicked second and her arms went around me and she let out a whoop of joy. I turned east onto the 62 and headed for more open road and third gear. Fourth and fifth came easy.

"Are you okay with this?"

She hugged me with her thighs.

"Does that mean yes?"

Another hug. Just the way I liked them. Comfortable now, I leaned back. Her arms relaxed around my waist and she settled her hands on my hips. I rested my elbow on her thigh and I got the feeling it wasn't her first time on a motorcycle.

Kate had done her hair in a ponytail, and occasionally it would get caught in the wind streaming past the big motorcycle's fairing. She caught it and tucked it down the front of her jacket.

I adjusted a mirror so I could see her reflection. My payoff was the huge grin. She caught me looking and leaned forward to put her lips close to my ear. "This is fabulous. Where have you been in my life until now?"

"How about if we make today day one?"

Mindful of our conversation a little earlier, I left it at that.

We continued east into the desert without saying anything. Occasionally, I felt Kate's cheek on my shoulder. It was her way of letting me know how much she was enjoying the ride.

Eventually, reality intruded. It always does.

"What time is it?"

I think we both forgot she had to be at work.

"I don't know. I never wear a watch."

"I have to get back," she said.

"There's a turnaround just a few miles east of here. We'll turn there."

I turned off the highway onto the gravel drive to the inn. Before I could get to the adobe, Kate stood up on the pegs, leaned over and kissed me on the cheek.

"Hey now. What was that for?" I asked.

"That's for next time."

I helped her get the helmet and chaps off.

"Can I change in your room?"

"Of course you can." I waited outside. "It's cold in there," she said.

"When you come back I'll have a fire going for you."

"I left my bag in your room. Is that all right?" she asked.

"You can pick it up after work," I told her.

"Will I see you for dinner?"

"You know you will, Kate."

She smiled and headed toward the restaurant.

"I like the ponytail."

She turned. "I'll see you later, Frank."

I just might hang around for a day or two until the weather warms up. In the meantime, I should have the fireplace blazing and the room nice and warm by the time later comes around.

Going Home Again

I was road-weary and sunburned from the day-long blistering sun that scorched my face and arms. Fifteen hours of dust and grime protected me from it to some extent. I reeked of asphalt perfume, as I called it.

It was past time to get off the road and relax. A shower and a meal would go a long way toward a new day tomorrow. I needed to start to think about funding for my ride south for the winter. Maybe I'd even look for a place to stay and a part-time job and settle down for a bit.

It had been a long time, but in another thirty minutes, I'd be in Clearwater one more time. I crossed the Kam River and in my mind I could see the vast lake in the southeast. I was a long way from the taco stand's waitress from hell, but that's a story for another day.

Fifteen years ago, I dedicated a day and showed up for a funeral. I hadn't been back since. All my close friends were long gone, like me, or dead. No family. Nothing left but vague memories since I pulled up stakes a lifetime ago. All of our crowd had left the one-horse town as fast as they could put it in the rear-view.

It was time to see what I left behind.

The road into town had changed a lot in those fifteen years. It was barely recognizable. It made me feel like I was somewhere else. Pizza parlors, restaurants and eat-n-pukes littered both sides of the street. There was no holding back the perception of progress.

I picked a gas station, pulled in, and fueled up.

I got talking with the gas jockey and he told me about a place to stay. It was about a mile away on a side street. He wasn't sure if it was still available, but it sounded okay. Clean, according to the jockey, and in a fairly new house.

I thanked him and thundered into the street. Since it wasn't so late, I figured on a drive-by before crashing at a no-tell motel. I could always go back tomorrow and rent the room if it looked to be worth it.

I turned off the main drag onto the side street and rode past the place. It looked good from where I sat—a newer two-story in an older neighborhood. There was a small garage in the back. Excellent. I reversed course, switched the ignition off and coasted up the gravel-packed driveway to the side door.

My intent was to walk around back to have a quick look at the garage. Instead, I got sidetracked by a woman sitting in the shade on a lawn chair.

"Hello," she said. "I didn't hear you drive up. You must be here about the room. I'm Sandy."

"Hi, Sandy. I'm Frank. Yeah, I'm here about the room. Someone at a gas station told me about it."

"Would you like to see it? Come on, I'll take you."

Sandy swung her legs over the edge of the recliner and leaned forward to stand up. I took the opportunity for what it was and gave myself a good look past the open top of her shirt and down into the freckled cleft between her breasts.

She looked up and smiled a shy smile. At least, her smile looked shy to me.

"The room isn't very big, but it's furnished with a bed and a dresser. It's right across from the bathroom and the shower."

She brushed past me with her head down and opened the door. "Come on in. It's upstairs."

I forced myself to watch the finest pair of legs I'd ever seen topped off by a pair of snug cutoffs proceed up the stairs ahead of me. Needless to say, I wasn't in a great hurry to get to the top. When she got there, she paused and waited while my eyes rose from her toes to her nose.

"It's on the left. I told you it wasn't very big." She looked at me with those dark-brown eyes and smiled.

I gave the room a once-over, but I already knew what I was going to do. "That's all right. I'll take it."

I went downstairs and out the door to my ride. Sandy followed. She held open the door and watched me unpack. It didn't take long. What I owned I kept in a couple of saddlebags. A rolled-up blanket held the rest of it.

"I think there's too much space in that room for all this."

She laughed. "Well, if you ever get the urge to add to your wardrobe, I'm sure there'll be room enough in that old dresser. There's a closet for you to fill, too."

Sandy let the door close behind her and I was left with a vision of her legs through the screen door.

I never had enough money to stay on the road for long. Paying the rent had always been a problem. When I made good money, it didn't help that my feet were always getting itchy for fresh sights and sounds just a little farther down the road.

I started the day with a local paper and a quick look at job ads. I discovered a couple scattered around the city worth looking at, but they didn't interest me much. Instead, I ended up walking an easy distance down the street to a hospital.

An old friend of a friend in the boiler room gave me a break. The job wasn't much—sweeping and washing floors mostly, and emptying trash bins. I didn't complain. It would pay the bills for a while. It would put some money in my pocket for the ride south in the fall in my quest to escape the cold for warmer weather.

Twelve-hour days at work didn't allow me to see much of Sandy right off. I wondered why she was alone in such a huge place, but it was none of my business. With her good looks and those shapely legs, she probably wasn't lonely, judging by the late hours she sometimes kept.

The long shifts I put in started to get to me. When a four-day stretch of R&R came up, I was more than ready for it. On day one all I wanted to do was relax and catch some rays. I grabbed my blanket, wandered out to the back yard and unrolled it on the cool grass.

I must have dozed off. When I came to, Sandy was standing off to the side, throwing the length of her shadow over me. I eased myself onto an elbow and checked out the tan on those long legs. My eyes traveled up to meet hers. On the way, they were sidetracked passing over the shadow of dark nipples showing through a sheer white shirt.

"Would you like something to drink?" she asked. "I made some fresh lemonade."

"That would be nice," I said, still giving her the once over.

"I'll be right back." She stepped around me to go inside. When I opened my eyes, there she was again, a vision sitting in her chair by my feet, staring down at me. She had switched out her shirt for a bikini top. A shadow of fresh lipstick graced her lips.

"You must have dozed off. I didn't want to wake you. I figured you needed your rest after all those late-night shifts you've been putting in. Would you like that drink now?" She poured out a tall glass and bent to hand it to me. I took a long, cool drink. I took a long, cool look, too. She didn't appear to mind.

"I like that. What's the secret?" She smiled and moved closer.

"Lots of sugar. The hotter the day, the sweeter the lemonade." She held out a hand. "It's too hot out here. Let's go inside."

I never had much of an ability to say no to a woman who offered it to me like that. I followed Sandy up the stairs. I already knew all about her legs. Judging by what I had seen on display in the back yard, I didn't think I'd be disappointed with what she had stashed under the bikini top.

Or anywhere else, for that matter.

Sandy made me wait by hiding her breasts with a forearm while she pushed her cutoffs past smooth, lean hips. There was no g-string to obscure the view. There was a nice, trim runway to land on, too. She dropped her forearm, but that's all that moved. Firm breasts with long, erect nipples greeted my mouth. By the look and feel of them, I knew they would be all I needed.

She dragged her breasts along the length of my thighs and took me in her mouth. Definitely a woman who knew what to do to please her man.

She never stopped until she had me completely drained. She didn't allow me to keep a drop. She pushed me back and climbed on. Her breasts bobbed and weaved and kept time with the rhythm of her hips. She pushed herself off and looked down to watch the length of me slide out of her.

She crawled down between my legs and took me in her mouth. There was no holding her back. She knew just how to work it, keeping just the head in her mouth. She tugged with her teeth, then her lips. Her hand held the rest of me against her hard nipples.

Just as there was no holding her back, I

couldn't hold back. Sandy was too persistent. She sucked, greedy, noisy, and I finally gave up. She milked the last drop out of me, licked her lips and came up for air to rest her head on my thigh. I grabbed her hair and pulled her up.

I kissed her and tasted both of us.

Come early morning and I figured I'd get back into my own bed. Don't ask why, but it probably had something to do with not spoiling myself. Reluctantly, Sandy agreed, but not before fastening her lips on me to make one last pass.

"I'll see to this at the next opportunity." She grinned and bounced out of bed and down the hall.

I didn't join her in the shower.

Sunup comes early to a man who's spent the night with only a glass of cold lemonade in his stomach and a warm woman by his side to feed his appetites. I wanted to get out and throw a leg over my ride before anyone else in the house was aware. I wanted to be alone with my thoughts, and I needed the wind and the early morning smells to blow the cobwebs out of my head.

Fool that I was, I left Sandy to her shower.

My ride started first kick, and I gently wicked the throttle and eased the clutch to start down the driveway. I figured there was no sense complicating my life by pissing anyone off with more noise than they deserved this early in the day.

When I got caught at a red, I waited until I could rip through the gears, exhaust roaring, bent on escape, impatient to be on the road. The asphalt ribbon stretched out in front of me like a woman's long, lean legs. The rising sun at my back painted the grass and trees a dark green, while the early morning light teased the western sky.

Beneath me, my long shadow rode between the lines like a man on a woman. The wind howled in my ears. In answer, the rich throaty purr of exhaust pipes roared in defiance. I threw my feet over the highway pegs, leaned back from the handlebars and let a huge grin plaster itself on my face.

The rising sun was barely over the horizon when I coasted into the driveway the next morning. There wasn't a whisper of a breeze. It was going to be another scorcher of a day.

I leaned the bike over on the kickstand, got off, and opened the door. Breakfast on the road hadn't been much more than a stop for a roadside leak. I hoped that Sandy's fridge would at least have a little more in it.

My tired, wind-weary eyes weren't prepared for what I saw next. Sandy was there, standing beside the stove. She had on the bottom half of an apron. That's all she had on. Someone had written Kiss the cook on it in felt pen.

"What would you like for breakfast, Frank?" she asked.

"Whatever you're serving up." I couldn't help myself. I smiled a shit-eating grin.

"I've never been on a motorcycle before. Maybe after you're fed, you could take me for a ride."

Does life get better than that?

I stayed until the fall and until the leaves started dropping like so much rain on a cold, windy day. I had a full wallet and a plan that took me as far south as I needed to get to sunshine, blue sky and warm weather.

I asked. How could I not? Sandy said no.

I rode off in the brisk, early morning darkness with an empty back seat. It was good riding. I got a thousand miles that day.

I never went back.

I never do any more.

Fast Food and a Slow Waitress

The 90s were the heyday of text-based chatting in rooms that, at best, barely allowed one to attach a .jpeg image as part of a post. Anyone logged in could remain anonymous and unknown, with only his/her chosen nickname or 'nick' visible to all. Video chatting was, mostly, extremely rare or unknown. Those text-only chat rooms predated the advent of face-to-face video chatting in real time that has since taken over and is now common.

Unbidden, the woman behind the counter revealed to me all in one long, desperate breath that she's eighteen and has a three-year-old at home. She doesn't look old enough, but she's pretty enough.

I think I must have misheard, and to be sure, I ask, *Three months?*

Wrong. I'm forced to listen to her declaration of stupidity a second time. If she is looking for sympathy from me, she is sorely mistaken. And by the way, thank you for letting me know how abysmally stupid you are.

Welcome to the land of the original fast-food restaurant. Where confession rules. Where the person taking your order bares her soul and tells all while you wait for your breakfast burrito and artery-clogging potato latke.

I continue to stand and wait, all the while listening to her interminable babble concerning the story of her useless, empty life. I think back to when I might have been the same age, and know that she would have been a loser then, too.

I'm tempted to ask her out, mindless as the exercise would be, just to shut her up.

Anticipating the next in line, I turn. There is no one. Trapped now, with nowhere to go, I put on a thousand-yard stare and pretend to be engrossed in this woman's mindless yammering.

Like the inability to make the choice not to look when passing a freeway car wreck, I'm unable to turn off my hearing. When she pauses to refresh her oxygen level, I smile and welcome the opportunity to move to an empty table.

"I'll bring it to you when it's ready," she calls out, and I turn to leave. I let her know I will be grateful for the small favor. I'm grateful, too, for the silence that envelopes me as I walk away.

I don't let her know that.

It was the end of my back-road solo ride through Amboy, Kelso and Cima. Since sunup, I'd ridden hundreds of early morning solitary miles through the desert, under predictable blue sky. With little to no traffic. Virtually no people. This northernmost loop was especially isolated.

It turned out to be a perfect ride.

Finally, I had found the perfect place, too, but it wasn't the only one.

I had decisions to make.

I had been searching. For months.

It seemed so easy at first. Be nice. Be kind. Be concerned. Listen to what they have to say. Just listen. That seemed to be the key. They all want someone to listen. It turned out that was the secret to gain their trust.

The problem was that the more I listened, the less I cared, no matter how anxious and hungry I became.

I didn't ask a lot of questions. Never pushed for answers when I did. Never expressed doubt. When whoever it was disappeared for a while, I did, too. But of course, I never really disappeared in the true sense.

I changed my handle.

I lurked.

And looked some more.

I found so many.

And discarded them all.

Except one.

The one that caught my attention. Whoever it was came in and out, always creating a fuss. A shit disturber. That's the way it looked to me.

Right from the start I suspected that whoever it was might be masquerading. Some will do that. Pretend to be male. The really lonely ones. The scared ones. Scared that they'll attract all the weirdos in the world.

Her appearances were irregular. Day after day passed and I would end up having absolutely no luck. I'd sign on under one of my many nicknames, sit back, lurk, say nothing. After an hour, I'd leave, pissed off and annoyed yet again that she hadn't shown.

Still, I wasn't certain. Whoever it was, was it a female?

There were some subtle clues. References to relatives and school and parents and the way she talked about them. By then, I convinced myself I wouldn't be wasting my time.

Even the handle she used.

Gracja.

It all came down to the name. A dead giveaway. I bided my time and ever so slowly began acknowledging her, for I was sure of that. Sure that she was female. I had no doubt. It would be only a matter of time until she would admit it.

Each time her nickname splashed onto the

screen it would be like starting over. It always took her some time to renew our acquaintance. Cautious at first. She was so cautious. I let her lead. I knew that if I didn't, she would disappear for good.

I spent hours in my attempts to gain her trust. Just when I started to think my time had been wasted, I learned it hadn't been after all.

Sometimes it was so easy. They liked to show off. Liked to show how smart they were. How witty and charming. How intelligent. And I do like the intelligent ones. The ones that do the instant analysis. Sure of themselves, so sure of their ability to make judgments about a stranger.

So sure and certain, they would bet their lives.

Gracja was like that. Always a quick comeback with some smartass comment thrown in for good measure. Sometimes I could barely keep up with her obscure references and jokes, and I told her so. That seemed to relax her even more. It allowed her to think she had won the war.

By now, we were long over our initial awkwardness, and there was an easy air of breezy informality to our online meetups. Of having been friends for quite some time. Together we had relaxed into it. Of course, we weren't friends in the normal sense, whatever that was.

Then slowly, finally, she began to break down.

>>>What's your name?
>It's right there in front of you.

I knew what she meant. On purpose, I was being evasive.

>>>No. I mean your real name. What's your real name?
>My real life name is Ben.
>>>Mine's Gracja. Gra-see-ya, is how it's pronounced.

There it was, at last. I had everything I needed. Now I could get busy. As I suspected, it was her actual name if she was Slavic.

>Gracja. Is it European? Polish?
>>>Yes, Polish. And I'm 20.

It didn't take me completely by surprise, certainly, but telling me her name was an obvious admission. I could tell she felt relieved. I knew I was. With her deception over, I could create an even greater measure of trust where little to none had existed before.

Finally, I had one. I wanted to say, I trapped one, but of course it wasn't quite like that.

Never so easy.

One step at a time, and step one was completed.

Certain of it, I could begin the proper work.

>So. You're a woman after all. You must have known I suspected.

>>>Really? You never let on that you knew.

>Of course not. Your secret is safe with me.

She attached a picture to her post. It was grainy, under-exposed, dark, but it revealed a young woman with long dark hair and a pretty face. I saw the mere fact of sending it as another victory.

>What color are your eyes?

>>>Blue. And my hair is down to my breasts.

Interesting that she used breasts and didn't describe it as being half-way down her back.

>You have breasts too? Then you definitely are a woman!

Then, suddenly, this:

>>>I have to go. I'll be on later if you want to meet up.

>We'll see. Now that I know who you are I

might get bored with your antics in here.
>>>No, you won't

She was gone.

And no. I won't.

I hid for several days. In truth, I didn't really hide. I changed my name—my nick—and that allowed me to be invisible. As such, I scoured the chat rooms searching for her. By lurking and staying invisible, I could spy and not be recognized. And, while doing that, I could kill two birds and scout for more possibles.

I liked to have more than one iron in the fire.

Finally I logged on with my usual name. Seconds later she was there. No doubt she had been lurking in the background with some inane name, as I had been. That was a good sign, one that showed she was definitely interested.

I smiled to myself.

>hey!
>>>Hola! where have you been?

That proved as much.

>I've been here and there. I'm like you. I don't talk to many people until they catch my

attention.

Thinking, unless I know they're female.

>>>do you have ICU?

That came out of the blue.

>yes, I do. Why?
>>>what's your number?
>you're a demanding wench, aren't you?
>>>come on, what is it?
>I don't give it out to strangers

Which was true. I had only four names on my list. All of them women.

>>>we could chat in private if you gave me your number

Unbidden, she sent hers my way. I quickly searched it and sent back an authorization request. Gracja returned it immediately.

>I'm doing this against my better judgment

Not really. I didn't give it a second thought.

>>>don't be so distrusting. I won't be able to bite from here

No, she certainly won't. She'll have to get a lot closer for that to happen.

>I have to go, Gracja, it's late and I have to work tomorrow

I signed off abruptly, not giving her a chance to say goodbye. She had done the same to me on more than one occasion. I wondered how she liked it when I did it.

I had her. I was certain of it.

She had to be lurking, waiting for me to surface. Surely she must have known that I might do the same.

It seemed as though it took forever. And just when I thought I was on the losing end, success. All the time invested started paying off.

She waited for that bit of attention. Waited for someone to listen to what she said, or wrote. Waited for me. Because she knew I would be the one to give her what she needed.

Those first four—and now five—names I had on my chat list testified to that.

There were some that came on-line, off and on, for the entire day, and into the night, too. Gracja usually came on in the afternoon, around three or so.

I changed my name so that I wouldn't be recognizable, and it worked. I outlived a number of characters on purpose. I began to get confused, even though I had notes. I kept a record of their names, the name I used with them and what I told each one about myself. When I lurked under an alias, I made notes of anything out of the ordinary when familiar names were on-line.

Hell, I started to feel as though I was turning into a real creep. For the most part, I didn't have a problem with that. I could care less what anyone else thought—not that anyone would be learning anything about it.

That was the beauty of the net.

No matter who or what you were, no one really knew for sure.

I stopped using all of my chat-room nicknames but one. Instead, I spent most of my time lurking.

Watching.

Waiting.

Gracja chatted a lot with someone named musiclover. I had seen some of his ramblings on music, and to be blunt, it didn't appear as though he knew what he was talking about. I had that discussion with others in the chat room who had seen his reasoning. They agreed.

Others Gracja chatted with were mostly fodder for her biting wit and occasional outbursts of anger. There were times when I watched her rage on and on at people, and yet I was still consumed with wanting to know her better.

Her irrational outbursts concerned me, but I let them pass. After all, no one is perfect. She didn't demonstrate any anger toward me. Every time I went on-line and turned on ICU, she greeted me with the same enthusiasm.

ICU was perfect for me. I could show myself only to those on my list that I wanted to chat with. We had our own private chat window. Usually I'd be greeted with a message or two, and after a bit I'd invite one of them to open a chat window for one-on-one.

Adding Gracja to my ICU list had perhaps been a bit premature. It had taken a much longer time to get my first four addresses, but I was sure it would work out for the best with her.

That tiny little chat window made it appear so much more personal. So much more attentive. Private, personal, attentive. That's what they craved. The attention. Someone to listen. Someone to ask the right questions. To give the right answers.

Someone who cared.

Or someone who pretended to care.

I logged on and lurked. No Gracja. I opened a second window and logged on as vagabond and there she was, just moments later. Finally.

>hey!

>>>Ola! Man!

>how have you been?

>>>good. but I'm tired. I have some long class days.

>What are you taking?

>>>sociology and psychology

>then you deserve to be tired. you'll be all right. it's nothing you can't handle

>>>I know, but it's nice to hear you say that. thanks

>no prob. I know you can do it. say, before I forget AGAIN, I'm taking off for a couple of weeks

>>>where are you going

>I'm riding down to southern California

>>>riding? As in by motorcycle???

I could feel her excitement through the screen.

>yes. want to join me?

>>>can I???

>what about school?

>>>screw school!

>you say that now, but when you're supposed to be graduating—

>>I know, I know. so how are you getting there?

>west to Montana, then south. eventually,

I'll end up in Buena Vista. In February I'll run down the Baja to Cabo

>>>shit. you are an asshole after all. don't tell me that. you're going to ruin me. will you be spending the whole winter down there?

>not at all. I'll put the bike in storage and fly back in a couple of weeks

>>>shit

>and if you're lucky

>>yes?

If you're lucky, I'll let you join me down there. You're right. Screw school. I didn't write that. Instead—

>yes. if you're lucky I'll find a cyber cafe and we can hook up

>>>don't tease me like that. I'll miss our chats

>really? no way

>>>yes. really.

>that's nice to know, Gracja. now I have to go

The sudden departure was one of her tricks. Let's see how it worked when I used it on her again.

>>>then just go away vagabond man. go away and don't bother me till you get back

>we'll see

Did I have her or not?

This too was the beauty of the net. You could have a different home page on a variety of free providers. Up to twenty megabytes of useless and made-up information on some sites. Fake photos. Fake words. Fake everything.

Fill out a questionnaire with lies and half-truths and you could be anonymous to anyone that you invite to view your handiwork. Tell the visitors anything, and they love it when they read it. They'll come back for more, time and time again.

I had already proved that.

Useless information. Outright lies. Who's to know? The beauty of it all, if one contact wasn't around, there was always another to fill the void of idle hours. Another to show how compassionate and caring I could be. One more to show how sensitive to their concerns I could be once they got to know me just a bit better.

I began to think that five names on my chat list were too many, although I hadn't heard from three of them for quite some time. That meant two definite possibilities. One for sure. The second one coming along quite nicely now that I had seen a picture.

Damn, this was going to be tough. I knew I had a lot of work to do with teddygirl. She was in the beginning stages, and I was hoping that a sympathetic ear tuned to her emotions would help to endear me to her. Certainly, losing contact with three close friends would help, not to mention the fact that now she knew that I could be sympathetic to her feelings.

Yes. Two was plenty.

One now.

One waiting in the wings.

A motorcycle pulled into the restaurant parking lot. Two women dismounted and came in to sit at a table next to mine. I remarked on the bike and we struck up a conversation over lunch. They were from Connecticut, just passing through on their way from L.A. Both social workers, they decided to take a three-day fly-ride to get away from solving the problems of others. They intended to travel a circle route through the wilderness and back to the city.

They sounded competent and talked the lingo, and it appeared as though they had been riding for a while. I volunteered to accompany them on their ride, and they agreed. They wouldn't mind a companion who knew the way through the isolated area.

The day turned into a perfect opportunity to dry-run a ride without a passenger. I played the tourist with the women and picked viewpoints and photo ops with strangers who had never before seen the countryside. I ended up accompanying them as far as their turnoff to canyon country outside the wilderness boundary.

When they took off on their ride farther south, they were happy.

As was I.

Rehearsal complete.

I had my plan of attack. The rest would fall into place soon enough.

Or so I thought.

Net denizens are an unpredictable lot. They appear in chat rooms for a few hours or days or weeks, then disappear to return under another nick, another incarnation. Sometimes you can tell. Spelling and grammar idiosyncrasies, jokes, expressions and sayings are there to be noticed by the attentive. Bide your time and they'll be wanting your attention again soon enough.

They can't resist.

Especially the women. Vanity. Pride. A need for attention. Who knows the reasons? They preen online as though at a bar or a party. It's a different preening, though. As though with each word they type cries out, "Look at me. I'm here. Pay me some attention."

And I do.

But never right away. No. That would be too obvious. Or so I thought. There were some who would open themselves up right away. Here's who I am. Want to see a pic? Want to know more? Talk to me now. I have things to tell you. Learn all my secrets.

No, those were never the ones. I was interested in the quiet ones. The ones who would sit and ghost. The ones who were a bit shy. After all, mystery is good, is it not?

So I would bide my time, day after day. Week after week.

I poured over trail maps. Read up on local geography and history. I learned about desert vegetation and threw in some animal habitat for good measure.

My thinking was that if I could show myself as knowledgeable, calm and reasoned, that would instill confidence. I would need to be comfortable discussing the desert in all its varied hues. Scorpions, for example. A North American scorpion is only poisonous to small children and people with heart problems, yet everyone thinks they're abject killers.

Yes, I definitely needed to dedicate the time to learning what I could about the local flora and fauna.

Memorizing it all was easy. Well, if the truth were known, I didn't memorize it all. Look at it this way: If you were going to visit a desert area from some unnamed city, what would you most be afraid of?

Every desert movie and book has the

standard scorpion scene written into it. The chance of any of these women knowing much more than that about the desert would be slim to unlikely. To be sure, they would be more concerned with dry skin and moisturizers.

So I read up on a few creatures in case one of them asked, and learned the basics about some of the local plants and trees so that I could appear knowledgeable and confident. And that, together with what I learned about the local area's history, should be able to do the trick.

I get sidetracked so easily now. Perhaps it's because I'm desperate. I needed a willing participant. That's right, a participant. Not a victim. That would come with time. I was sure of it. Waiting and watching would be the tough part. Up to now, it had always been thus.

I waited patiently. I logged in under a variety of names and ghosted. I watched. Sometimes someone would ask if anyone had seen me.

I kept lurking and said nothing.

Night after night. Day after day. I logged on and lurked. Nothing. Other chat rooms came up blank too, although I remained hidden so as not to give myself away.

Then finally teddygirl broke the silence.

I had been teasing her about a pic for so long. It wasn't really serious teasing, just occasional comments about wanting to know what she looked like. A month ago she had sent me two pictures, finally. The first was of a plain-looking, dark-haired girl wearing glasses, her hair tied back, seated on a sofa.

Nothing special.

But the second? Wow. Shoulder-length hair, no glasses. It was taken outside. She was in front of a back yard fence. What she was wearing, though, was absolutely stunning. The top of the short blue dress only hinted at the lovely full breasts lying beneath. And as I moved my eyes lower, a pair of gorgeous legs greeted my hungry eyes.

Perfect.

I remember telling her so, because she was embarrassed to be revealing so much of her legs.

I tried to put her at ease right away after she sent me the two pictures. It was plain that she was unaware of how pretty she really had become since the first picture was taken. The usual You'll need a stick to keep the boys away and How many guys ask you for help with their homework kind of stuff.

But she only laughed, and said nothing like that was happening.

>what fools they are. let me do the talking and I'll straighten them out about you

I was only half joking. It became evident that she was modest about her looks, so I eventually let it be. She got my point, in any event, because of the way she thanked me.

>>>* hugs and a kiss on the cheek *

An email showed up from her telling me that she had another picture of herself in an even shorter dress. I knew I had to see this one, too. No matter what.

I sent back a short note right away, joking about her email. About how she was certainly getting over being self-conscious about how she looked.

Anxious, I was eager for her reply, even though it was really Gracja that I was truly interested in. Where was she?

Being her fickle self, no doubt.

The bitch.

Zahara. It was the name that caught my eye. I wondered whether she was attempting to evoke the desert. If so, it was working for me. From the beginning, I couldn't tell how old she was.

>>>zahara wrecked her car

Talking about herself in the third person. What the hell? I waited for a response to show up from any of the others in the room.

Nothing.

>what happened, zahara?
>>>I was turning off the main road and skidded sideways into the guardrails
>is the car a complete wreck?
>>>yes. totaled
>when did this happen? recently?
>>>about half an hour ago
>holy shit, girl. are you all right?
>>>yes. I'm okay. my head is a little sore, and I have a headache, but that's all. oh, and my ribs are sore too
>did you get a concussion?
>>>nothing like that. the paramedics came out and checked me over but I'm all right
>that's a relief. are you sure you're all right? headaches aren't good things to have after wrecking a car, you know
>>>yes I'm fine. thanks for asking though

That's how I met her. A drama queen if there ever was one. We kept bumping into one another in the chat room from time to time. She had a sense of humor and her spelling and grammar were pretty good—which is a plus compared to some of them.

At least she wasn't illiterate.

She told me she liked to write. Poetry, mostly. Probably bad poetry, I thought. Even so,

I sent her one of my email addies and asked to send me a poem she had just finished. She hesitated at first, but relented and said it was on its way.

Gotcha, zahara.

Zahara's poem was quite a piece of work. Very sensual. I had to learn more about this one, and keep her interested as best I could. I didn't want her scurrying away until I found out how old she was.

I stayed offline for several days, and then finally I responded to her email about the poem, telling her exactly how it had made me feel about her. That I thought she was a very sensual person. Quoting from her poem and giving her examples of why I thought so. At the end, I asked if she would like to meet me on-line to talk about it.

Sure enough, the next day, I had a response telling me to meet her in the room at ten that night.

I entered late, but only by five minutes. No sooner had the prompt popped up saying that I was in, and there she was.

>>>hiya!
>hey! it's good to see you again
>>>I've been looking for you here. where have you been?

>I've been busy. I haven't been in that much. but I'm here now
>>>finally. I can tell you liked my poem
>yes. you know I did zahara

I knew her name was Beth, from the email header, but I would wait until she volunteered the information.

>>>I've never shown anyone my poems before. I was worried you wouldn't like it
>you got my email, didn't you?
>>>yes, I did
>then you know how much I liked it. you really opened yourself up to me when you agreed to send it
>>>I know I did. I couldn't help it. after I read what you wrote and put up on your web site, I couldn't get it to you fast enough

Zahara was talking about a site I kept on the web. I pointed certain people there and left it up to them to decide if they liked it or not. There was a story up there, and a couple of poems I patched together to try and encourage some expressiveness from those who saw it.

All of it was shit.

>so you liked what I wrote?
>>>oh yes!
>it's sweet of you to say, zahara, but I like

your writing better than mine. do you have any more poetry I can see?

>>>that was my best one. I have some others, but I'm not ready to show them to anyone yet

>well, when you are

>>>I know. you'll be the first

>zahara, can I ask you a question?

>>>yes. I'll tell you anything you want to know

>do you work?

>>yes I do. I work in a restaurant.

First hurdle down.

>tell me about yourself

>>>okay. I'm 5'7". brown hair green eyes. small hands, slender wrists.

Slender wrists?

>>>and I have to go in to work. I'll see you next time.

>yes, you will.

>>>oh, and my name is Beth.

>all right, Beth. good night

I didn't see zahara again for several more days. She sent an email, telling me she was busy with work, and I took it at face value.

The few times we chatted were brief. Either she was just leaving the chat room or I was just coming in, or it was the other way around. We punctuated those times with brief emails back and forth. Sometimes flirty, sometimes not.

Then this cryptic email message: "I'll be home later tonight. Why don't you give me a call around 10:30?

She signed her real name, followed by a phone number.

I logged off.

I already knew I'd be calling. The area code was in Vermont. She was an hour ahead of me time-wise. I waited until exactly the correct time.

The phone rang once.

I looked hard at the blond fast food server when she showed up at my table with my order in the almost-empty joint. It was difficult to tell, but beneath the uniform it appeared as though she might have a body hiding out. Maybe she wasn't so bad after all.

"How long have you worked here?" I asked

"It's my third day. I'm still nervous. It's my first job, too."

Well now. This was getting interesting. "Who babysits when you're working?"

"My sister. We share a place."

"That's nice. You're lucky," I told her.

"Do you live around here?" she asked.

"I've got a place out in the desert. Why?"

"I just wondered," she said.

"Are you seeing anyone?" I had to know.

"No. Not right now."

No doubt the boyfriend disappeared at the prospect of being trapped by a teenager with a baby.

"So what are you doing when your shift is over later?" I asked.

"I have to get home right away," she said.

"Do you think your sister might put in a little more time for you after work?"

"She might. Why?"

"Then let's go for a ride when you get off."

"I'll call her."

Nancy. Her name was Nancy. She didn't bother to change. She scurried out of the fast food franchise wearing the clothes she had on when I saw her in the morning. She jumped on the back like she'd been doing it for weeks. She brought the odor of leftover French-fries with her.

I attributed her eagerness to new-job jitters and thinking she might have a man in her life instead of the boys she was accustomed to. At least, that's what I told myself, because I wouldn't have it any other way.

"Let's go."

She barely managed to get her foot on the other peg, not yet settled on the back.

"Sit, bitch." I let out the clutch and she flopped back into the seat and giggled. I eased out onto the main drag and headed east.

Her lips moved against my ear. "Where are we going?" she wanted to know.

"Do you like surprises?" I wanted to know.

"Sometimes."

"Then you'll have to let me know how you'll like the one you're going to get."

The young ones are like that. Way too trusting. You might as well put a ring through their nose and lead them around like a cow to the slaughter. Except you wouldn't need the ring.

They would just follow.

Anywhere.

I headed off the highway and turned onto the wilderness road. I followed the asphalt to the turnoff for my campsite. It sat far back from the main road on a rough sand trail. Isolated. All by itself.

There was nothing for miles in the surrounding desert.

I stopped the bike in front of the tent and Nancy got off and unzipped the fly.

"Not so bad. Can I go in?" She didn't wait for an answer.

I walked around the site, looking for the tracks of anyone who might have been interested and nosy enough to walk or drive up. There was nothing. Everything was as I left it.

"Are you coming in or what?" Nancy was impatient.

Scattered clothes at the foot of the sleeping bag greeted me. Nancy lay naked on top. By the time I finished undressing, she had her feet in the air.

Her legs parted to welcome me home.

I didn't mind the leftover French fry stench so much.

It's dark when I come to. Nancy is in the same position she was in when I crawled off of her. Perhaps not exactly the same. Her feet are back on the ground, but her knees are still spread. Her grunting has quieted, replaced by an occasional dreamy moan.

For a minute I think I'd like to climb back on while she's still warm and sleeping.

Or maybe not.

Instead, I pull on my boots and step outside into the cold air of a starry desert night. On my way past the firepit I pick up the shovel and continue into the darkness. A hundred feet beyond the tent, I start digging.

Cold sweat runs off in rivers and drips onto the dry sand. I barely notice.

"What are you doing?"

Shit. She must have followed me. I step back from the edge of the pit.

Naked Nancy no longer reeks of French fries. Instead, the sheeny lather of sweat she wore earlier has rinsed away the stink. Now she just smells like she's going bad.

Is that even possible? A woman with a best before date stamp on her ass? Now there's a concept. Personally, I thought they already had a best before date. For me that worked out to be about five days past when they first fell into the welcoming position with a willing look and parted legs.

A roundhouse swing and the shovel sees to it that Nancy's best will never expire. In the dark, she doesn't even see it coming. She drops into the hole without making a sound. I don't even have to drag her.

So much for this one's best-before date.

I hum to myself and fill in the hole. When I finish, I dress, break camp and head on down the road.

In my haste I almost forget her clothes.

Half a dozen miles later I pull over and scrape out a shallow depression. The still night air briefly fills with the sickening odor of stale French-fries. The stink lasts about as long as it takes to scoop sand on top of the pile of clothes I leave behind.

Dead Man's Hand

The last time I saw Jean-Marc alive, he had on a noticeable and unique ring that he picked up in his travels. It was in gold and silver, extremely detailed, of a tall ship, fully rigged and under full sail, on what appeared to be black onyx. I have never seen anything quite like it before or since.

When I asked about the ring, he told me he found it during one of his market forays into the Merkato in Addis. The souk where he bought it had no one who was able to tell him anything about it.

I wanted to look at it more closely. When I asked him to take it off, he refused. Obviously, it had a great deal of meaning to him, and to some extent, I understood why, given the intricacy of the design. Where he bought it probably figured into it, too.

In any case, I thought the ring summed up every aspect of our occupations as aviators. We wandered around the world to wherever the jobs took us, mere transients, moving from place to place, crossing oceans and continents, going contract to contract, and moving from relationship to relationship with women we would never see again.

The nature of our chosen profession scattered the outfit's employees far and wide across the country and the world. It was a rare occurrence when any of us ended up back at the head office in a group. When we did, we liked to get out on the hanger floor and mingle with the maintenance people responsible for the well-being of the aircraft with which we entrusted our lives and the lives of our passengers.

If the right crowd was in town, some of us would end up hitting the hotel down the road for an evening well-spent until closing time. The hotel owner was a former company employee. If he was in a particularly good mood, he'd lock the doors and allow the drinking and partying to go on well past closing time and into the wee hours of the morning.

Plenty of tips kept one or two of the waitresses interested, but only enough to encourage them to serve more alcohol. Not a one of us ever convinced any of them to go home with us or to go out on anything resembling a date. Perhaps through experience they had grown wary of spending time with anyone involved in the transient world of aviation.

One of the maintenance crew that usually came along for the beer was young Bill, a lowly apprentice. He was a slow-witted, slow-talking, slow-moving man who spoke with a drawl that managed to irritate the hell out of anyone who spent too much time listening to him. Consequently, he had been labeled as not the brightest bulb in the hangar, so to speak.

Bill had a wife who didn't take kindly to his evenings spent out on the town with the boys and the resultant absences from the dinner table at home. Following a night of drunken debauchery, he would drag his sorry ass back into the shop on a Tuesday or a Wednesday or a Friday morning. He'd appear with a hang-dog look and a ready tale about what his wife had done to punish him for his indiscretions the night before.

I don't recall any of us ever telling him we thought of his wife as a first-class bitch.

Eventually, we became fed up with listening to Bill's constant whining. It was really starting to drag down the celebratory atmosphere in the bars we all frequented as a group.

After one particularly long and winding nighttime trail of devastation and destruction, we ended up at a strip club to close out the evening's entertainment. When the place shut down after last call, some of us pulled Bill aside in the parking lot to give him a pep-talk before sending him on his way to his merry wife.

With our words of encouragement freshly implanted in Bill's tiny brain, he was no doubt eager to test our advice. He eagerly departed for house and home, where we all knew he would be chastised by his bride one more time. His tardiness in arriving would most certainly result in bringing on wifey's disagreeable disposition and shrill tongue yet again.

Following this most recent episode, Bill didn't show at work for a couple of days. When someone finally noticed his absence, we chalked it up to phoning in sick, and our coffee-room discussion ended soon after.

Larry, the owner of the company—in his own right not to be outdone as a drinking machine, along with the rest of us—called Bill's bride to inquire if he was ill. Unfortunately for Bill, this was not the case. Upon hanging up the phone, Larry came out to let us know Bill had been hauled off to jail.

A quick call to the precinct confirmed it. One of us was dispatched to bail the man out. Bill was back on the shop floor once again. This time, he had an even sadder tale of woe with which to regale his comrades.

It seems that our pep-talk of a few nights previous had really cheered Bill up and put him in the proper frame of mind for the coming confrontation with his blushing bride. Upon his arrival, he discovered his belongings had been deposited on the front porch.

The door was locked. The message was clear.

Bill, not one of the smartest flies circling over the horse turd, pounded on the door for a couple of minutes. Not getting the response he hoped for, and by now thoroughly fed up, Bill applied force and shoulder to the locked door.

Unfortunate as it was for Bill, his wife had condescended to open the door at the exact same moment. Both door and Bill landed on top of his bride. Woman that she was, she didn't take too kindly to this turn of events and consequently, when the police arrived, Bill was hauled off to jail.

Now you know how Bill's mind works, or doesn't, as the case may be.

We were all somewhat chastened by the unintended consequences of our advice-giving. Nevertheless, it afforded us a good laugh at Bill's expense.

The overseas project I headed up needed a third aircraft to cover the increased workload. The company boxed one up and had it flown into Djibouti on the Horn of Africa. It arrived via an Air France 747.

I delegated myself to getting the import documents completed. This proved to be a nightmare until I discovered the appropriate French official. He recommended the proper amount of baksheesh with which to anoint the palms of the overly officious locals. This encouraged the release of the aircraft from customs bond.

All that we needed was an additional pilot to crew the helicopter.

When the charter arrived and Jean-Marc stepped onto the tarmac, I was as surprised as he was. He had been with the outfit for almost as long as I had. We last worked together on forest fires in northern Canada, but we had never spent time in the same foreign locale.

His base had been Ethiopia. Consequently, on his R&Rs he went into Addis to scour the markets there on the lookout for interesting and unusual bits and pieces of gold and silver for his female acquaintances around the globe.

I, on the other hand, preferred the more isolated regions on my rotations out, and consequently ended up in Mog, or Djibouti, or Galkayo, to name only a few. I preferred those places to getting to know the white enclaves in the larger centers such as Nairobi or Jo'burg, where one could become enmeshed in the local white perceptions of the continent's native affairs.

For the most part, I figured there was no point in going to Africa to see and experience a white world. Africa was black. Its former name on the old charts was the Dark Continent, for the unknown and mysterious visage it presented to the European explorers of the 19th century. I didn't want to miss out on any of that, even if it was the next century and things were starting to modernize.

Don't get me wrong, though. I enjoyed all that Nairobi had to offer, too. In fact, when I could get there, I ended up spending quite a bit of time with an Israeli girl. I recall the first time I took off my long pants before settling in her bed. She took one look at the tan lines on my thighs and said, "You live in the desert." She wasn't wrong about that.

It took some time to get caught up on all of this, of course, and so Jean-Marc and I would retire to the local watering holes where we could sit and observe the local color. Mostly these spots were frequented by a few Djibouti regulars, la légion Étrangère and various and sundry other miscreants as could be found.

At one point, we discovered a troupe of misguided German flight attendants trapped against their will with their flight crew during a grounding. We managed to rescue them from their boredom and brought them into the fold.

We spent ten days trolling the depths of Djibouti depravity with our new-found friends. When our aircraft was finally assembled and ready for departure, we said our goodbyes to the women and flew off into the rising sun and lonely desert.

Eventually, the contract we were on ended and we all went our separate ways yet again.

I lost touch with Jean-Marc after our African adventures. Occasionally I would end up in some of the places he had been, and I would be approached by someone or another as to his whereabouts. I didn't know, of course. We were still being dispatched wherever the company saw fit to send us in the far-flung outposts in the world of helicopter aviation.

It was during one of those assignments that I learned Jean-Marc had been killed while on a flight in mountain terrain. It seems he had run out of airspeed, altitude and ideas, all at the same time.

I didn't get many of the details right away. Eventually, they trickled down to me via phone calls to the company and the various people I knew in the business. Jean-Marc hadn't stood a chance. He ended up smacking the ground with a substantial thud.

I did learn one thing though, and that was Bill—no longer young—had been his swamper on that job.

Many years later I decided I needed something different in my life to maintain my sanity. I retired from active flying and tied myself to a desk. I was still involved in aviation, but I was finished with the flying.

Some would call it flying a desk.

Occasionally, I'd see one or two of the old

crew who came to town to do a job. Sometimes someone passing through wanted to touch base, and we'd tell lies about old times.

Then, to my complete surprise, half a dozen of them showed up on an aircraft headed west. Their charter flight had stopped for fuel and maintenance. To kill some time, they all wandered across the field to my air tanker base office.

Bill was one of them, standing in the background. Finally, he walked up, and we shook hands. To my surprise and discomfort, I noticed he was wearing Jean-Marc's ring. Without blinking an eye, I now sized him up for the man that he was: A thief. A liar.

And finally: A grave-robber.

I wondered. Had he removed the ring from a dead man's hand? Or had he merely put it in his pocket when he collected Jean-Marc's personal effects?

The former would be no surprise to me. The latter was unlikely. Bill told me himself he had been the first man to arrive at Jean-Marc's accident site.

For me there was no doubt Bill removed the ring from a dead man's hand and claimed it as his own.

Bank Robber Dames

I'**ve spent forty years** riding the highways and by-ways of North America and Mexico. I met people I liked. I met people I didn't like. Most of the people I liked best were women. It was no contest.

Some women ignored me. Some didn't. Some comforted me. Some gave me grief.

Sometimes, but not often now, I wished the ones that gave me grief had ignored me. They're the ones I call my bank-robber dames.

Just about all the significant women in my life turned out to be dark-haired and dark-eyed, with only a couple of notable exceptions for dishwater bottle-blonds that never mattered in the grand scheme of things. Four of them scared the bejesus out of me, and those were the darkest-haired and darkest-eyed of all.

The first, when I was in my late teens, was a little hippie girl with flowers in her long, straight hair. I figured she probably ironed it, although I never saw her doing it. Perhaps she got up in the middle of the night to keep her secret.

We would get to talking, and always after a while she would bring up how she'd imagine things to be for the both of us in one of her futures or another. Eventually, I figured out she wanted to settle with a man and have a family. A factory job in the only game in town wouldn't hurt, either.

I tried to convince her otherwise, but it didn't work. It was not for me to stay around and trapped. I didn't want to end up old and dead and buried only a mile from where I grew up. I was too intent on completing my rendezvous with my future and the world.

In time I made good my escape. I always felt as though it was a narrow one.

I learned from that, but not much, for what man ever does when he is young?

The second was a married woman, although strictly speaking, with her sharp gray, not brown, eyes, she didn't qualify to the fullest extent. That didn't matter, though. All the signs were there. I still was incapable of recognizing them.

By then I was a fire pilot trapped in a town with nowhere to go for amusement on my R&Rs.

The day was hot and sunny the first time I saw her. She had her hair tied back with a purple scarf. She was pushing her son down the street on his tricycle. Something about the picture attracted me, and I remember thinking, *I like that*.

I saw her around town a couple of times after that. Eventually, I caught up and wrangled myself into position to meet her. Before long, we were dancing together in the dark, and in the daylight, too.

Once the fire season ended, I started traveling with freelance flying in the off season. It took me away often enough and long enough that each time I returned, it was like coming back to a new and different woman.

This time it was me who thought about a future and all the rest to go with it. She wouldn't budge, though. She could see me for who and what I really was—a footloose vagabond aviator without roots. She knew in her heart that I would never settle down.

She was right, and we both moved on, but not together.

Eventually, I did settle down into a flying job on the Dark Continent. It was there that I forgot all about her. That experience was one of the best things that ever happened to me—and by that, I mean for both forgetting her, and for experiencing Africa, too.

It was just what I needed to clear my head of my time with her. Even so, the method certainly left something to be desired. It did temper me, though.

Years later, I returned a changed man. Many of the things I saw and did would remain with me, untold, for a lifetime.

Some secrets are meant to be kept. Who was it said, "Never confess on your deathbed. You might live long enough to regret it?"

So I kept secrets. I still do.

Many years and relationships had passed by the time the third dark-haired beauty came along. I was working in an old-school motorcycle shop in one of southern California's high deserts.

It was her first day at work. I saw her walking through the doors of the shop's sales floor. She was on her on her way to motor clothes. She looked straight ahead. Chin held high. She had to have felt all eyes on board. Those eyes were well-deserved. Long black hair that swayed with every step. A purposeful stride. Dark bangs over deep brown eyes. Bright red lipstick that suited her perfect pale white face. A plum sweater. Leather pants. Jacket draped over a forearm and a bag hung off a shoulder.

She was beautiful. All of her.

By then I knew the signs by heart and did the best I could to ignore her. Oh, yes, I was nice and polite and joked and laughed with her, but I tried to keep a distance between us. I even gave her a nickname—la bonita. I never revealed that to anyone.

It wouldn't have been prudent.

Keeping the distance was difficult. She was smart and funny and serious and when she talked, her eyes would sparkle. Her hair would shimmer in the light and sway just so when she walked. It truly was difficult, but I managed. Somehow.

Until I couldn't any longer. Neither could she.

Although, sometimes, even today, I wish we hadn't.

Then she left town, and I left town, and that was the end of that.

Until the day I learned she had been shot in her bed while she slept. Her empty-headed husband made a sad attempt to claim it was suicide. Five minutes in the interview room had him bawling his eyes out and confessing. That got him 23-to-life.

Beloved Delissa left behind two daughters and a world to mourn her loss.

Regrets.

I have a few.

The fourth came along when I was least expecting it, for isn't that how it usually happens? I looked through an open door and there she was, a rather plain-looking young woman. There was something about her, though.

I tried to ignore her, too. Our weekly work schedules overlapped for only a couple of hours on a couple of days. I stayed on the edge of the group she hung out with at work. She kept her distance, too, and I was happy with that.

Until she didn't.

She came to stand beside me. Leaned back against the same wall. Said hello. For some reason, it pleased me very much. Even so, I kept my back pressed to the wall, as if that would save me.

It didn't. One's back to a wall only prevents escape.

We wouldn't face each other when we talked. Rather, our routine was to stare with the same faraway look, across the same open space, out past the tarmac that stretched before us and led to the world beyond. It became obvious to both of us we were kindred spirits.

Then, one day while we were standing around killing time and pretending not to flirt, I detected the faint odor of perfume. It was just a hint. The way I liked it.

I should have walked away then.

I didn't.

Instead, in that instant, I surrendered.

Somehow, she knew.

I asked, but she would never tell me the name of that scent. I would look for it, but I never found it. She must have secreted it away after discovering how it had caught my attention.

I called her Chica, and she seemed to like that.

I told her things I never told anyone else. The good things. About the Southern Cross visible in the dark African nights. How the sun would rise and set fast across a flat desert horizon. How the dim of twilight on the flat equator would last for never more than a few minutes.

I left out the stench of burning flesh and death and starvation and other things best left untold.

Eventually, she was the one to leave—yes, imagine that. She was the one who flew away. She caught her future mid-flight and moved on. I let her get away, a regret so late in life. I knew I had no other choice, for it was the sensible thing to let her do at her young age.

We could have held on. We both knew that, and we both knew too that it would be only for a while. I already had my life. Hers was just beginning. I would not keep her from her own rendezvous with life.

I miss her still.

I'm pretty sure I don't have time for a fifth, but if I do, I won't say no.

Ah, yes, my bank-robber dames. I almost forgot.

Had any of those four said, out of the blue, "Let's rob a bank," I might have turned, and looked, and asked, "Only one?"

More Bad Girls

A good day for a ride

Frank was in a hurry to get to Nogales and la frontera. It had been a long day in the saddle. He was fresh out of Mexico and ready for a break. Shade, cold water and a quick gas station burrito were all heavy on his mind when he pulled into the gas'n'go in Valle Verde, north of the border. What he ended up with was something else entirely. He wanted to get out of town in a hurry, but chance and a local woman were working against him.

1

Butterfly by Crazy Town. I remember the first time I heard the song. I was on the road, heading north out of Mexico for Nogales. I turned off Mexico 15 for the old Hermosillo-Nogales highway at the cutoff by Aeropuerto

Internacional. I'd crossed there many times.

The semis were always backed up for half a mile or more in advance of la frontera. Usually they ended up blocking and filling all the access lanes on the Mexico side heading for U.S. Customs.

I ended up winding my way around the smell of idling diesel exhaust and hot rubber and overheated brakes. That there was never a breeze in the stifling heat didn't help. Most times, the drivers would wave me ahead and slow or come to a halt to make room so I could ride past.

When lane splitting didn't work, I crossed over the wrong way in the southbound lanes and took it from there. The odd time a trucker wouldn't let me in, I gave him the finger on the way by. I made sure never to come to a stop in front of one of those guys.

If you can't imagine why, you don't do much long distance riding.

Off on the west side of the divided highway, the campesinos rested in the shade where they could find it beneath skimpy, stunted trees and shrubs. Manned up and relaxing by their campfires, they were waiting for dark to do what they had to. In a few hours, those same trees would be abandoned and lonely. The campfires would be smoking embers, waiting for the next day's marchers on their way to the promised land.

That would be the last rest they would get until they wormed their way on foot across la línea into the hell of the desert to the north on their way to their destination-if they even knew where that was. Unless they happened across water spotted out by someone sympathetic to their dreams of a better life, it would be a long, thirsty trek, fraught with danger. Sometimes ending in death.

Some would join family members already waiting eagerly. Others, not so fortunate, might be alone and scared while they waited for their ride once they made a successful crossing.

I was always anxious for my own turn in the lineup. Dusty and dry as dirt because my last water was done hours ago. Hungry. Tired. Road weary. Eager to get across. Even more eager to get home.

Nogales. Usually no wind, not even a light breeze if I remembered right. Hot. Stinking exhaust reeking of diesel.

For amusement while I waited my turn in line, I watched the Border Patrol literally heave the illegals back onto the Mexican side faster than I could count. Extradition, U.S.A. style.

Screw 'em if they couldn't take a joke.

When my time came, I pushed back my sunglasses. I wanted to look the border agent straight in the eyes. I liked to let him know I was just happy to be there. Sometimes he'd commiserate with a laugh or a smile or a knowing shake of the head as he waved me through after a perfunctory passport scan.

I crossed at Nogales a bunch of times, and it was always the same. From Nogales it was a 475 mile hop to California and home. Easy. I could do that standing on my head, but always by Valle Verde I'd be looking for cold water and fuel.

Even so, it was still a good day for a ride.

I didn't see her drive in. She must have been there already. I would have noticed a woman in an old Dodge beater that was some color of brown too faded by relentless desert sun. The windows were down. No air conditioning. Maybe it stopped working sometime in the last two decades. If it ever worked. The left front was definitely low.

Maybe she was doing the same thing I was doing. Looking for a little shade and some cold water before heading off to somewhere else. I caught her out looking over my ride parked on the shady side of the building.

Maybe it was the bedroll tied onto the back that drew her attention. If she was smart, she'd notice the back seat occupied by my small duffel. Maybe it would help her figure out I was riding solo. Beyond that, I left it up to her.

Long dark hair. In a ponytail. I liked that. She turned around and I could see it was braided, too. Down to her waist. A nice rear end at the end of it from what I could see. I'd need a better look first, though. I drew closer. She glanced my way. I couldn't see her eyes behind the sunglasses.

She smiled. I nodded and smiled back and pushed my own eyeshades back on my head.

A white shirt with the long sleeves neatly rolled up above her elbows and dark pants and shoes covered off all of her. Too bad. I wondered, though, because even in the plain clothes she looked pretty good.

But then, I was coming out of Mexico after spending the winter.

Maybe she was headed to her shift in a bar. Or maybe a reception of some kind. I didn't ask.

"Would you help me? I can't get my low tire filled and I have to wait tables. I'm going to be late," she said.

It was plain enough. I'd seen her struggle to get the tire aired up. Maybe on purpose. So what, I figured. She wasn't so bad looking. A few freckles here and there, covered with a bit of makeup. Nothing too extravagant.

She handed over the air hose. The movement revealed the inside of her arm. Covered in track marks. Up and back down. Scarred. Old scars. No scabs. Definitely not fresh by any stretch.

"You're all right now," I said. "I can tell."

I don't think she knew I noticed. Her eyes

flicked over me as I finished and stood up.

"I'm definitely all right now. And thank you."

She stood in front of me. Not moving. Like she was checking me out. Maybe her experience working in bars told her I was all right, too.

"It's going to be dark soon. There's plenty of animals on the road at night in these parts," she said.

"It's been a long day in the heat and I'm about wrung out," I said. "I'll take a break, get some water, and carry on."

"You out of Mexico?" she asked.

"Si."

She smiled. "No hablo. Poquito."

"So which is it?" I asked.

"Poquito."

She pushed her own sunglasses onto the top of her head. The movement revealed soft brown eyes. I liked eyes like that. It always made it easy to tell a lot of things about a woman if I could see her eyes. I took another look. I think she did, too.

Her eyes were clear. Her pupils looked to be normal. I already knew mine were bloodshot. Eight hundred miles of wind in a biker's face will do that. The rest of her still looked pretty good, too.

"When did you eat last?" she wanted to know.

The question was plain enough. I must have

looked the sight. I never thought I ever looked hungry, though. "Probably this morning sometime. I've been on the road since before sunrise. Where you off to?"

"I'm working a reception. There's usually a few no-shows. If you want to eat before you head back out on the highway, I could probably arrange it."

"That would be all right. I need a break anyway. It's been a long day for sure."

"You won't be allowed in the kitchen. You'd have to stay out back. You could eat, though, if you wanted. I'd make sure you did."

"As long as there's plenty of water. Give me a minute, okay?" I fetched the key and headed for the men's. I splashed a little water and dried off and minutes later I was good to go.

"I'm Karolina."

"I'm Frank Ross. Pleased to make your acquaintance, Karolina. That's a pretty name."

She ignored that last. Maybe she heard it too often from some and had been disappointed.

"Follow me." Karolina and her beater shook, rattled, and rolled over the curb and out of the gas station lot. I ended up following her to a large banquet hall. She stopped in the huge parking lot out back and popped the trunk. "You can put your things in there."

Maybe I wasn't her first biker after all.

"Walk around the side when you're done. It's in the shade. I'll prop the door open and tell

José to watch for you. If it slows down, sometimes they let us bring out chairs for breaks at the picnic table."

Sure enough, José showed up for his break and I introduced myself. He offered me a smoke. I shook my head and he sat down and lit one. José must have gotten along with Karolina, because he treated me pretty good, too. He brought out water and iced tea and even sat down for another smoke. We chewed the fat, me with my poquito Spanish and he in pretty good English.

"She's been talking about you, señor," José said.

"Call me Frank. What's she saying?" I was interested for sure now.

"Only that you helped her get here on time. Her boss doesn't like it when she's late."

"Is Karolina late a lot?" I wanted to know.

"Not since she dumped el diablo."

Now I was paying attention. It seemed the two were better friends than I first thought. "El diablo?"

"Her boyfriend," José told me.

Thanks to a customer who never showed for the banquet, I dug into a plate of chicken fricassee. I dug in like a man who hadn't seen food in a week. My table manners went out the window and I was glad there was no one watching. Then José popped out to see how I was doing, and I was forced to slow down.

I gulped water to wash it down and thanked him again. Karolina had to be playing at hard to get. She still hadn't stuck her head out the door.

Karolina's twin in the form of a beater the same faded color as hers, screeched into the dimly lit lot. He made it on four wheels only because the driver was smart enough to stomp on the brakes and slow down. Metal squealed until he let up on the brakes and got out. The door was just loud enough to wake the dead.

And maybe wake the devil, too, according to José. "El diablo, señor Frank."

"Gracias for the warning, José. De nada. It's nothing."

"Que?"

José hurried inside, probably to warn Karolina. He was too late. Instead of looking forward to digging into the fricassee for the second time, I was confronted by el diablo screaming Karolina's name from halfway across the parking lot.

I set down my fork and pushed back from the table. I stood up and stepped in front of the screamer as he was about to reach for the door. "You probably shouldn't do that. The person you're looking for is working. You don't want to get her in trouble, do you?"

"Up yours, asshole," el diablo insisted.

"The asshole's name is Frank. Pleased to

meet you, too." I stuck out my hand and made like I wanted to shake his. The confused look was just what I hoped for. I swung a roundhouse into his gut that put him in stop mode.

Diablo backed up a foot or two and put up his fists, thinking it was going to be a boxing match. Then the fancy footwork began and I wasn't about taking chances.

Just in case, I let fly with a foot between his legs. The dancing stopped. He dropped to his knees like a rock and kept on going until he lay doubled up on the asphalt. Both hands grabbed at his crotch. Red-faced and huffing and puffing, it was all he could do to groan and stutter.

"Now be nice, dipshit. When José comes out, I'll send him for Karolina."

I dragged my new friend over to the table. I put a foot on his head, fished for the automatic peeking out of the back of his pants, and tucked it into my own. That should have told me something right there.

Trouble is I only wanted to finish the fricassee. It was tasting pretty good to a man who last had breakfast on the road just past sunrise.

Karolina must have known better than to come out and spend time with me while her ex was still hanging around. She halted at the doorway, looking all concerned. I grinned and winked like I was seeing her for the first time.

"What's for dessert?

She didn't hesitate for even an instant. "If you get rid of that piece of shit stuck to your boot, you can have just about anything you want."

At the beginning of the day, my plan was to ride north to Phoenix to touch base with an old lawyer friend. We went back a long way. I still owed her a pile of dough, though. Isabella would have to wait. I was pretty sure she wouldn't be brokenhearted about it, mostly because she didn't know I was going to look her up.

2

Karolina's **boyfriend was beginning** to get antsy. It could have been my boot on his neck. I removed my foot and let him struggle to sit up. Together with José we helped him stand and eased him in the general direction of his car. I waited for José to depart in a hurry.

"You might want to think about ruining a woman's chances at her job. You don't look to have a whole hell of a lot to offer her if she loses it."

I pushed him behind the wheels and slammed the door. He put pedal to metal and raced out of the lot the same way he arrived. A few minutes later, I caught Karolina peeking out the banquet hall's open door. With her ex run off, she joined me out back on her break. She brought cake and ice cream and half a plate of chicken for herself.

"Thanks for that," she said. "I'd be getting fired if it wasn't for you."

"Thank José. He's the one warned me. I couldn't have you getting fired before I got a chance at dessert, now, could I?"

Karolina peeled off a spoonful of ice cream from my plate for herself. She put spoon to tongue and worried at it for a bit until it melted and I think I could almost see the wheels turning.

"I've got a place out in Sahuarita. It's not very big. There's plenty of hot water and there's a small spare room," she said.

I waited her out, and she went on.

"You know. If you need a place. For a bit. Temporarily."

Yeah. And if Karolina needed someone to punch out her boyfriend later, that would be me. I wondered how many handguns he could put his hands on.

"Is that your way of telling me I need a shower?"

She smiled.

"Well, according to you, you've been on the road all day." She smiled across the table again. "You kind of have that scent of dust and sunshine and asphalt about you."

Result. A woman who recognized it for what it was. "You ever have a biker boyfriend?"

"My dad. He rode."

"Ah. A good man. Maybe the three of us can go for a ride sometime," I said. Which was about as much of a promise as I'd ever make in this lifetime.

"He died when I was little. I remember the smell, though. When he came home from a ride he used to pick me up in his arms and hug me."

"I'm sorry, Karolina."

"It was a long time ago," she said.

She wasn't so sad. She had to be over it by now.

"We'll be done in another hour or so. You going to hang around, Frank?" she wanted to know.

"I could." Like I'd be leaving before the second course.

"Then I'll see you after cleanup."

I waited patiently, mostly because I used my jacket for a pillow on the picnic table beside the building. I must have caught at least a couple of hours by the time Karolina and José came out and let the door close behind them.

Karolina greeted me at the table t make sure I was awake before she made off for her junker parked beneath the lot's single light pole. I kept an eye on her just because she was long-legged and walked with a certain gait special to all the girls I ever knew.

Her junker wouldn't start. The engine turned over one time and then the starter began its clicking sound. No one could come up with cables so she threw a leg over and climbed on the empty seat like a pro. She settled back and hung on tight. Her thighs squeezed and her arms went around snug.

Not so tight that I was about complaining. That I ever would.

Karolina leaned into me. Her lips moved against my ear, giving directions while making wordless promises. I wondered if she'd keep them while she gave directions to north of town.

The trailer was old. Not so big. My single headlight played over the side and I could tell it was sunburned and bleached out just like her car. She waited for my signal. I steadied my ride before she eased off. I dropped the kickstand and joined her on the hardpack desert sand and gravel.

Karolina walked up three steps and opened the door. She reached in and flipped a switch and the inside lit up, revealing neat and tidy. Everything had a place. Dishes were put away. No piles of papers and unpaid bills littering the counter or the table. No laundry stacked and drying in piles or thrown over furniture. She wandered down the short hallway turning on lights.

"The bathroom is down here. I'll put out a towel for you. You go first and then I'll have mine."

"Why don't you go ahead. It's your shower. You've been on your feet all day. I've been sitting down."

"All right then. One more thing, though." Karolina hesitated.

Here come the rules, I figured.

"The handgun tucked into your belt. You planning on doing anything with it? Like rob a bank? Or a drugstore?"

I raised my eyebrows. To be honest, I'd forgotten all about it.

"Yeah. I wondered what was digging into me in all the right places and making me happy, so I pulled up the back of your shirt and checked." She grinned and I thought maybe.

"That belonged to your boyfriend," I told her. "I took it away from him before he could hurt himself." That was my story. I might stick to it. I might not.

"It figures. He never did get the gift of brains god gave to most other men. And he's my ex boyfriend. Just so you know."

"He didn't get the message, did he?"

"Nope. Not so far."

I slipped the magazine and checked the action. One in the chamber popped onto the table. "He was prepared, I'll give him that. Does he chase after you often?"

"Not so much any more. I would have lost my job if he made it into the hall tonight, though. Old people don't like seeing stuff like that." Karolina headed off to the shower. She exited in a shorty robe and a towel wrapped around her hair. No pretense there.

It was my turn and I didn't take long before I changed into clean jeans and a fresh shirt. I felt good after breathing asphalt and road dust all day in the heat.

"You clean up not too bad, stranger." Karolina took her long legs and her shorty robe down the hall. She returned looking good in shorts and an off-white blouse. It set her pale skin to glowing. Like most women, I think she knew it, too.

"You don't look so bad, either," I told her.

"Thanks. You want to sit outside and help me count the stars?" Karolina didn't wait for an answer. She opened the fridge and pulled out two bottles and led me out back. Judging by the setup, I figured she did that a lot. Chairs and a table and a chiminea, an outdoor fireplace, sat forlorn and alone.

She pulled her chair beside mine and handed me a beer with just enough sweat on it to make it feel good when I swallowed.

"You mind if I run my ride back here? If your ex gets to driving by and doesn't see the car, maybe he'll think you aren't home."

She followed me around the front. I untied

my bag and held it out for her.

"If you're looking for it, it's in my bedroom," she said as she took it inside.

She looked good walking away in those shorts. Long, shapely legs climbed the steps. I waited until the door closed before I pushed my ride around back. I didn't wait for Karolina to show up.

My bag wasn't the only thing I found in Karolina's room. She was sitting up in bed, reading. A single faint light illuminated just enough to encourage me to keep going. Long, dark hair tumbled over bare shoulders and fanned across the white pillow as backrest.

Karolina leaned over, placed the book on the night table, and pulled the covers aside.

"You were asking about dessert a while ago. You should probably turn on the air conditioner before you dig in."

I turned on the air conditioner.

The a.c. rattling in the window was doing its job too well. I climbed out of bed and switched it off. I left Karolina sleeping peacefully and pulled on my jeans in search of a beer before heading out back to wonder at my good fortune.

It was good fortune, or the devil was playing his usual game with me.

Soft footsteps crunched on the hardpack

behind me, approaching slowly. Karolina. She probably thought I'd crawled off in the night like a coyote.

"I'm still here," I announced. "Look at how bright those stars are."

The empty chair scraped across the gravel and I pulled it closer.

"You'll need a blanket. It's cooled off a lot."

My chair tipped sideways. I saw more stars close up before I collapsed on the sand. I was freezing cold on the ground by the time I came around. I staggered into the trailer. The bedroom was empty and Karolina was gone. I didn't need a note to tell me her jealous ex was the responsible party.

I started in the small kitchen and came up with a list of numbers taped to the fridge. José's was near the top. I finished dressing and was about to make the call when the door opened and Karolina walked in.

"Where the hell have you been? What happened? Where did you go? I thought your ex had taken you," I told her.

"When I woke up you were gone. I didn't see your bike. I forgot you moved it. I put on some clothes and walked over to José's place. They're friends of mine. I thought-"

So we were both still here. That was a plus.

"I got up and went outside to look at the stars. I thought you woke up and were coming out to join me. That's when I got a rap on the side of the head that laid me out like cold meat in a reefer. I thought-"

"You thought. I thought. It's cold out here. Let's go back to bed and talk about it while we warm up."

Karolina shook me awake. I checked the clock. The numbers were holding steady at 0530. She flipped on a light and I squinted at the dark window, then back at her. My eyes wandered and stopped squinting at the same time.

"Can't a man recharge for a bit longer? Yesterday was a long one for me, in more ways than one."

"No, silly. I have to go to work," Karolina said. "If you play your cards right, I might even cook breakfast."

An image of this woman dancing naked in front of a frying pan full of bacon took over and I climbed out of bed to dress. I turned in time to get a glimpse of a fine, silk-covered ass being ruined by a loose white skirt. A white blouse covered up the rest of her that the bra didn't.

"I thought you were going to make breakfast." Disappointed, I almost crawled back into bed but for remembering that Karolina's car was broke down at the hall where we left it. "Right. I'll start the bike."

Karolina hiked up her skirt to climb on the

back, revealing the finest pair I'd seen in a while on a gringa. The Mexicanas weren't so bad either, though. Except this one was climbing on the back of my bike, and I'd just left her all too warm bed. In my book that made her número una.

She put lips to my ear, like she did last night. "You didn't get to look last night. The lights were out. Disappointed?"

"The only thing disappointing me this morning is that I had to leave your lovely, warm body and bed and take you to work."

"You can come back after you drop me off." Her lips repeated last night's motions against my ear. This time, they took me to the small diner where she worked. She made sure to give me another show of gorgeous thigh when she climbed off.

"You coming in?"

To say Karolina looked disappointed when I told her I had things to do would be an understatement. I think she must have thought I'd be collecting my things before heading on down the road. Except I wasn't.

I recognized José through the diner window and waved before riding off to the banquet hall and the woman's car. I raised the hood. A quick look at the mess of a battery and I went off to retrieve a cheap version. I popped it in, fired up, and Karolina's car was good to go.

Back at the diner, I let José know the car had

been fixed. I settled in at the counter to be waited on by one of the most beautiful woman I ever had the pleasure of looking at. In my absence, Karolina had put on just a bit of makeup. She left off the lipstick and instead had put on only a little lip gloss. At least, that's the way it looked to me.

"What're you having, biker boy?" she asked, as she sidled up to me.

"Can I have more of what I had last night?"

José appeared out of the kitchen, grinning. "No, señor. We don't serve fricassee."

Karolina blushed a bright pink. José and I laughed and laughed some more. The customers didn't know what the hell was going on, which was probably a good thing.

"José, if you know what's good for you, you'll get back in the kitchen or I'll tell your wife," Karolina threatened.

I slapped hands with José and he disappeared.

"Frank, you're getting eggs easy, sausage, and hash with a tomato side. Like it or lump it," she told me.

"Great. Can I have dessert later?"

Karolina didn't miss a beat. "Pie with a side?"

"I fixed your car. It was the battery. I replaced it." I handed over the keys and wondered what kind of dessert that would get me.

"In that case, I get off at three. You can have dessert at my place."

Karolina bent a finger and motioned for me to move closer. I leaned over the counter. She bent, put her lips to my ear, and whispered. "The only thing on the menu will be me. And I won't be on my side."

It was my turn to blush like a schoolboy. I caught José grinning at me from the other side of the pass-thru.

I waited out Karolina's shift at the diner. When it ended, I pushed the empty coffee cup across the counter. Together, we headed outside to my ride. She hung on tight and I think she must have had a grin pasted on her face all the way to the banquet hall at the prospect of picking up her car. I knew, because I kept checking out her reflection in the mirror.

The smell was something else. By the time I got to the empty lot, the stench of burned rubber and gasoline fumes was overwhelming. I knew it wouldn't be good. I was right, too, when we rounded the building and the smaller worker parking lot in back.

Karolina's car was a smoking, burned-out, empty hulk of metal reeking of gasoline and the stink of burned rubber.

"Damn, Frank. I can't afford another one. That son of a bitch-"

"You think it was your boyfriend?" I got off the bike and took a better look. Broken glass was scattered beneath the gas tank. By the look of it, it was a Molotov cocktail that did the job. "Yeah, I think you're right. What do you want to do?"

"What I want to do is go pick up that gun you left at my place and teach the son of a bitch a lesson."

"Well, I can't have you ending up in jail. I'd have to bring you dessert, and believe me, it's not the kind of dessert we've been serving each other so far."

"I know, Frank, but damn it-" She stomped her foot in frustration, hiked up her skirt, and climbed onto the back of the bike. "Let's go home."

I waited for Karolina to get out of her work outfit. She changed into a pair of blue jeans and a shirt. I held out the helmet I found in a closet. "You want to go for a ride?"

"You're making me wear one? Where's yours?" she asked.

"All right. You win, stranger." I pulled my old helmet out of the trunk and put it on. "Let's ride."

Karolina climbed on the back like the pro I knew she was.

I hesitated before punching the starter. "You need to show me where your ex lives, girl."

"You're not gonna do something stupid, are you?"

"Not unless I get caught, baby."

The boyfriend's yard was filled with an RV and a couple of boats. Two new trucks sat in the driveway. A brand-new car squatted on the curb. Which begged the question: why was he driving a wreck when he chased Karolina down at the banquet hall?

"You want a car or a truck?" I asked, only half serious. Her comeback was quick.

"The car, please. I'm not a truck girl. And just how do you plan on putting your hands on that car? I don't want to be driving something that's stolen."

"How is he funding all of it?"

"Drugs, most likely," she said. "Or illegals. All the while I went with him I never knew him to have a job."

"Yet you worked every day."

"Yep. That I did. I can't be sitting around all the time. And I won't be having any kids to keep me in jail at home. Just so you know in advance."

Yeah, there wouldn't be much chance of that happening. At least, not right away. "You need to tell me everything you know about the ex. The sooner, the better if you want that car. I want to know why he drove a beater out to the banquet hall with all those new vehicles parked on his property."

I took Karolina home and she called José. We ended up invited for supper. Showered and shaved and fresh out of bed, we walked to José's place. We took our time, arm in arm, hips bumping hips. It wasn't far, but it took us forever.

"You want to go back to bed?"

"Yes." There was no hesitation.

I halted.

"We can't. José is expecting us any minute."

Karolina knocked and a short woman answered the door. Two little kids hovered at her waist as I was led in by mom and Karolina, who introduced Lupita.

"They'll soon stop being so interested and give you some space."

"It's all right. I don't mind."

I shook hands with José and Lupita gave me a hug. "Karolina likes you-"

"Lupita. Don't tell him that. He'll never leave." Lupita cluck-clucked.

José and I exchanged glances. "Don't worry, Frank. She told me the same thing at the diner."

"Well, I kind of like her too. Plus she makes a mean dessert." I winked in Karolina's direction. Her face and just about everything else flushed.

"We're having American tonight, Frank. Lupita figured you probably had your fill of Mexican food all winter and you're ready for some down home cooking."

"Well, that's about half true," I told him. "I can eat my fill of either by now. Whatever Lupita wants to do is fine by me."

What Lupita wanted was for José to put the ribs on the barbecue and finish them. I followed him out to the back and slid the door closed. We settled in with a beer while he lit a cigarette and took a long drag.

"What's the deal with Karolina's ex, José?"

"What do you mean?" he asked as he took another drag and let it out.

"Karolina told me he's never worked a day, yet his yard is full of toys. What's going on? Drugs?"

"Maybe. But mostly I think it is illegals. You saw what it was like when you crossed la frontera, no? There are rumors he promises jobs for money. Once they get across, some are sent to him."

"And you know this for a fact?" I asked. I wanted to be sure.

"I think I can say, si. I have many friends who talk about him that way."

"So then, he's a people smuggler. A coyote."

"Not so much that, maybe. But definitely he takes money and promises jobs. The jobs don't pay so much, or end up paying nothing."

"And they end up working for no pay, nothing. Then he's a thief, too. How long did Karolina go out with him?"

José looked toward the door, checking for

Karolina. "I think for a couple of years. She had lots of money to spend for a while. Then they broke up. I don't know why. She ended up in the trailer you see her in. And with the wreck she drives. They must have had some problems."

I'd seen that already. "Someone torched her car in the banquet hall lot."

José answered too fast. "Si. That sounds like something he would do."

"There was broken glass under the gas tank," I told him.

"Yes. He likes that method. From what I have been told."

Lupita rapped on the glass and yelled out the window. "José. Check the ribs, por favor."

"Best not keep the wife waiting, Frank. Time to eat."

3

Flashing blues in the rearview jolted me out my good-fortune reverie. After all, who but a cop could put a damper on a biker's dream of being in the wind and hassle-free? I kept my hands on the handlebars, just like I did every time it happened. There was never any sense tempting fate.

"Get off the bike. Put your hands behind your head."

Here we go. "Which is it, officer?"

"Don't give me backtalk." Obviously a man of few words.

He pulled the trigger on the taser. Twin probes inserted themselves into my back forcing my body to spasm. I ended up on my back on top of my motorcycle. I pissed my pants, rolled onto the ground, and lay still.

"That'll teach you to disobey a command from a police officer." For good measure, he gave me another jolt and I went spastic on the ground. Wonder of wonders, but I managed to keep my mouth shut. Either I woke up on the wrong side of the bed and bumped into a wall, or I was in a bad dream.

It turned out to be neither.

"You're under arrest."

"What's the charge, officer?" I figured I should at least know that.

He zapped me again. When I managed to get my shit together, I asked again. I got zapped once more for my troubles. This dumb shit just didn't get it, and that was fine by me. Maybe I didn't, either.

I struggled into the back seat of the cruiser and settled in nicely to attempt to empty my bladder. There was just enough to wet the seat.

My mouth stayed shut all the way to the cop shop. It wasn't a matter of choice. My teeth were chattering too hard to do anything but breathe. On arrival I was ushered into a cell straightaway.

That was a new one on me. I asked for a phone.

Nada.

I asked for a lawyer.

Ditto.

Three days and three meals later, someone had the smarts to let me out. My bike was waiting for me in front of the station. I turned on the key and discovered a full tank of gas. I checked the trunk and saddlebags. My belongings were loaded. I was good to go.

The voice behind me didn't instill any measure of confidence that I'd get away without taking a beating. "Get out of town and don't come back."

I looked across my bike at the familiar ox wearing a badge and a gun. It was the same one that pulled me over and decided on the spot I was guilty. Of what, I never did find out.

"You think it's going to be that simple? You've been watching too many old westerns, dumbass. You'll be hearing from a lawyer. Any lawyer. Because any one of them—even a local law school loser—will take my case and we'll both end up millionaires. Now go screw yourself, Officer Dumbass."

The stupid son of a bitch hauled out his taser and zapped me again. When I stopped twitching, I was back in jail. Jesus, but it was a new century. Didn't anyone watch the news any more?

Then I thought they were probably too busy drooling, watching cop shows at the chief's house, drinking 3.2 beer, and all of them too stupid to have a thought.

I got out a week later, six meals thinner and only a little smarter. My first phone call was to a lawyer I used to know in Phoenix. I'd been on my way to see Isabella when I got sidetracked by Karolina's flat tire. Isabella told me she'd drive down as soon as she cleared her calendar. In the meantime, she made me promise to keep out of jail.

"You won't be committing any obvious crimes, will you, Frank?" Isabella made sure to ask.

I laughed and told her she knew me better than that. I didn't bother trying to explain what I'd been through. She wouldn't have believed me anyway. "None that will stick after lawyering up with you."

We had a good laugh, but how she did it, I didn't care.

It was close to quitting time when I made my way to the diner. I backed it in and shut down. Karolina's surprised look greeted me as I took a stool at the counter.

"Frank. Where have you been? I thought you left. What's going on?"

The look on Karolina's face went from surprise to shock to amazement as I detailed my experience with the local PD. "You can't be serious. Frank. What the hell?"

"Oh, I'm serious all right. Not only that, but someone went through your trailer and made sure to load all of my belongings onto my bike before handing it back to me when they let me out."

That part got to me. Who and why was a mystery to Karolina, too, until she stated the obvious. "It has to be my ex."

I was beginning to believe her. Was it so far-fetched to take it from smuggling illegals to paying off the police to look the other way? Probably drugs had something to do with it, too. Karolina's ex was proving to be more than just a minor annoyance at having any kind of relationship with the woman.

Karolina promised pie and ice cream. While she delivered, José spotted me a mug of coffee, creamed and sugared just the way I liked it. While José and I waited for the woman to fill us in, she busied herself with clearing dishes and wiping tables.

"Are you ever going to stop and sit and start talking, or do we have to tie you down?" I asked.

And then I started my own wondering. Should I stay, or should I move on? It was what I usually did when things got dicey and I didn't want to play any more.

Isabella would be pissed if I rode off while she was on the way to meet up. She'd be even more pissed if she missed out on the false arrest case she thought I had. I'm sure it was the dollar signs, but even so, I owed her. Big.

"What can you tell me about that ex of yours?" I asked. I washed down the pie by sucking back on the coffee José refilled as we waited more or less patiently for the woman to begin.

"Randy was the high school football star. Every cheerleader wanted him. I got lucky." She laughed.

"Take a look at yourself in a mirror, woman. He's the one that got more than lucky to have you. Right, José?"

Karolina blushed. "Oh Frank. Stop it and let me finish before quitting time." She looked at the clock. "I've been traveling back and forth with José. Thank goodness he's a neighbor. Anyway. Which reminds me. You have anywhere to stay?" She grinned.

I grinned right back. "Well—"

"At quitting time you can take me home and unpack for the second time. José won't mind in the slightest if I don't catch a ride with him. Right José?"

She never did finish telling me about Randy.

Karolina settled onto the back of the bike like she belonged there for the ride home. We rode to her place the long way. I made sure to pass by her ex's. I cracked the throttle just for spite to let Randy know I was back in town. No one rushed out to wave a fist. And even if he did, I'd have only held up a finger while I rode on by.

I hoped Karolina would be good for me again. She certainly was the first time. I had no reason so suspect otherwise now. I deposited us at the end of her gravel driveway. Just to be sure I hurried in to check the fridge. She'd seen to it that it was stocked, so I dove in.

Karolina devoured my eggs and bacon and toast and I was in like Flynn one more time.

"You're a good cook, too. You're hired. When can you start chipping in on the rent for this dump? My surprise hid behind a smile.

"Any time you want, baby. My stash is in my handlebars. I'll get it for you tonight."

"You won't have time tonight," she insisted. "I have plans."

Karolina dragged me into the shower, and her plans for tonight went out the window by late afternoon. By eight, we were fast asleep. At midnight, we were wide awake. Karolina's elbow was stuck against my ribs and she was banging on my chest with a fist.

The loudest banging was coming from outside. Someone was beating on the side of the tin-clad trailer.

"Good grief, girl. Is there never any peace around here for a tired biker? I just got out of jail, and now it's like I'm right back in with the cops rattling nightsticks against the bars to keep me awake."

"Frank! Frank. Are you in there? Frank?" A woman's voice. And it was loud. I stumbled out of bed and opened the door.

"Put some pants on unless you don't have company."

Behind me, a naked Karolina poked her head out the door. "You can keep your pants on, darlin'. The man has company," she told Isabella.

"Which is why you don't have any pants, if I know Frank. I'm Isabella." She held out her hand and the women shook on it.

"Come right in. We won't be a minute," Karolina told her.

I disappeared with Karolina.

Isabela shouted after us. "Jesus, Frank, do you ever answer a door in your pants?"

Karolina's head shook and she grinned. "I think there must be a story there, but I'm not asking."

That pretty much sealed it. The box of wine came out of the fridge. Water glasses followed. I left for bed when the cardboard box was only half empty. When I woke up, the two women were cackling like a couple of witches while Isabella pretended she could cook. It looked like the women would be friends for life.

"Sit your ass down, Frank. We have some things to discuss," Isabella ordered.

"Do I have to eat your cooking?"

"Only if you don't want to go back to jail."

Karolina laughed her ass off before heading out the door to catch a ride to work with José. "Try to get along, you two," was her parting shot at both of us.

Isabella retrieved her briefcase, and we commenced getting into it. By the time she finished, I'd signed every piece of paper she put in front of me. I didn't bother reading any of it. To say that I trusted her would be an understatement.

"Frank, I'm telling you now. Unless you die, you're going to clean up. This local PD is a disaster of incompetence and ignorance and just plain stupidity on the part of the chief and all of his relatives on the force."

I must have looked doubtful.

"You're right to look at me like that. It's not going to come any time soon. By the time this works its way through the courts, you just might be an old-timer."

"In that case, I have nothing but time on my hands. Do I have to stay here?"

"Hell no," Isabella said. "But I think you'd disappoint Karolina if you left too soon. Why not stick around for a while and enjoy yourself?"

Which made only a little sense. Since arriving, I'd spent more time in jail than I had enjoying Karolina. "In that case, I need to know more about someone."

I gave Isabella the name of Karolina's boyfriend and his address and left her to figure out the rest.

"I'll be in a motel for a day or two digging up what I need to know on these clowns," Isabella said. "Stay in touch."

"In that case, join me for a real all-day breakfast feast at the diner. You still can't cook worth shit."

She couldn't, either. I'd been subjected to Isabella's cooking on a number of occasions over the years. We laughed about it now, but I didn't know how to take it at the time. I just ate it and shut up.

"And judging by the way you two look at each other, you're not going to be cooking for me."

"Not on your life."

We were in the process of finishing up. I was looking forward to breakfast at the diner with Isabella in tow. The best part of it all was I'd get the woman to pay, one way or the other. A healthy tip for Karolina wouldn't hurt, either.

Maybe I was counting chickens. Maybe it was my bad luck. I don't know. But when the door flew open and four cops stormed into the trailer, Isabella and I had time for a quick glance before the shit spread pretty evenly between us. It didn't take either of us much to figure out that something wasn't right with the locals.

They forced me to watch as Isabella was handcuffed in the trailer and led out to her Cadillac. The trunk opened and she ended up forced into it. She didn't struggle, wisely I figured. A uniform slammed it shut, got in the driver's side. Tires spun in loose sand, creating a cloud of dust over the rest of us.

It occurred to me that the cloud descending on the local PD was about to be a lot worse than dust if I knew Isabella.

Handcuffed and loaded into the back of a black and white, I wondered if I'd be heading back to jail. Before long, I knew. It was a short, familiar drive. That and the cell was becoming much too familiar.

The volume cranked up on the television in the PD ready room carried into the cells in the small building. Judging by the lack of acknowledgment that they had hit a home run by threatening Isabella, it sounded like they were more than a little dumbfounded.

They were finding out firsthand the abilities of the lawyer I hired to do my bidding. Writs of habeas were handled by her law partner in Phoenix and were presented to a federal judge. It was like she had a premonition of some sort.

Of course, the live video feed of our extraction from the trailer coming from her camera'd-up car didn't hurt. That it was recorded onto hard drives back at her office only made the proceedings go a lot smoother.

Even with all of that preparation on Isabella's part and the commotion it caused, I ended up serving another day. This time, there was no meal. Obviously the county was on an economy drive.

The beating I took from a couple of hard-core impostors sent in to share the cell left me wondering when it would end. It was obvious that Randy had more than a single in with the local PD. I left the cop shop wondering if the entire force was related.

There was only one way to find out. I parked on a hill and staked out Randy the ex-boyfriend's place in the rental I picked up. Binoculars and burritos stood in for José's diner cooking and the comforts Karolina had to offer at her trailer.

Randy's nocturnal comings and goings were like clockwork. By the time I had it down, I was more than ready.

I waited until Randy drove off in his fancy new half-ton. I couldn't be certain on the dimly lit street, but it looked like him. He was walking out of the right place. He looked to be the same one storming the banquet hall a few weeks ago.

Satisfied, I took a stroll around back, kicked in the door, and brazenly walked in.

I had no idea what I'd find, but I was in it for the duration. I wandered from room to room, flicking on lights as I went. Searching for something, anything, that might keep Randy off of the police radar. The only thing I came up with was a photo album. A quick look told me everyone in it was family. Everyone in it was on the police force, too. Isabella would have a field day with this information.

I tucked the album under my arm and walked back the way I came in. The lights went out before I managed to flip a switch. When I came to, I was in the middle of nowhere. A huge bonfire lit up the surrounding desert. In the firelight, I spotted the front end of Isabella's Cadillac.

If she was still in the trunk, she had to be a mess by now. Would she still be alive after sitting in the desert heat locked in her trunk? There wasn't a thing I could do. I was busy taking a beating administered by two of the deputies while Randy looked on. The smug look of satisfaction said he didn't have a care in the world.

"Leave him for now," Randy said. "That should be enough to discourage him. "I have to get back to town. There are people arriving that owe me money, and I intend to collect. If I don't get paid, neither will you."

I ended up slammed to the ground. My wrists and ankles stayed handcuffed. If I wanted to walk away, I couldn't do it. I was left alone with Isabella's car. There wasn't anything I could do for her but pop the trunk. She crawled out with an automatic in her hand and a bottle of water with a nice sweat running down the sides. She handed it over while she unlocked the cuffs.

"I was in a similar situation a few years ago," she explained. As if that was good enough, she went around to the trunk for another bottle. She cracked the top and guzzled. "I learned to be prepared for the fool who thinks he's threatening me by keeping me alive. Now get in. We're going back to town."

Those poor townie sons of bitches had no idea the hell they unleashed.

4

In Isabella's absence, raw CCTV footage of her escapades at the trailer and in the desert had been uploaded to her web site. A computer guru she had access to edited the footage. The guru had to be a wizard. It took some bit of editing to compress and then assemble the elapsed times between the interesting parts.

When it was ready, the final version was

forwarded to local television news. All of the stations played the same loop over the dinnertime news hour. Even the radio stations were carrying a version, although somewhat diminished by the lack of a video stream.

Isabella's phone rang non-stop. She answered the questions and filled in the reporters about the ordeal she and her client was put through at the trailer and out in the desert. Of course, all of it was couched in the language of lawyers. I heard the words allegedly and possibly and a few opinions thrown in for good measure.

Through it all, she stayed calm. I don't know how she did it. I was ready to rip heads off, but she knew that wasn't a solution.

"The only thing anyone will understand is a lawsuit, Frank. Doing what we both want to do would be the worst thing possible. I know that. You should, too, by now. Just look where we are."

Isabella was right, of course. Between us, we managed to experience more cop grief than a black man out for an after-dark walk in a white neighborhood. The question was, how long would it go on before someone put a stop to it?

Isabella took us to the diner where Karolina greeted us with hugs and fresh coffee when we arrived. "I thought you two had eloped until I saw the news. I'm glad you're safe."

Isabella plopped into a booth and cracked

her briefcase. "Frank wouldn't do anything like that. He already knows I can't cook worth a damn. And he makes some mighty shitty coffee, too, so we're pretty much even on those scores."

Karolina's eyes moved in my direction. "So that's why you always cooked. No wonder I had to get up to make the coffee. You wouldn't drink your own."

Talk about hitting a sore spot. I held up my hands in surrender while the women grinned. "You know, it's not nice to laugh at someone."

"We weren't laughing at you, Frank. We were laughing with you."

Isabella pushed across another sheaf of papers. I signed like my life depended on it. And maybe it did, but now Karolina had been dragged into it, too. She would need some protection from Randy, her ex.

"Now then, Karolina-" Isabella explained restraining orders and how they worked—or didn't, as the case may be. At the end of it all, Karolina signed without question.

"Let me remind you. It doesn't mean that they'll stay away from your place. If someone breaks the law—she looked at me like I was the criminal—they have every right to pursue whoever it is. And they can still make shit up."

"So what's changed?" I asked.

"They know we're onto them. If they haven't figured it out by now, they're dumber than a box of hammers," Isabella said.

Given the way the local brownshirts were treating us, I figured they were a bit short of more than a few boxes of nails, too.

"I'm headed back to my office. If you two need-"

Karolina interrupted her. "You better text me when you get back to the city. Or else."

She didn't say or else what.

Karolina's shift ended and she hiked up her skirt and climbed on behind me. Being the man that I am, I never got tired of a woman's long, shapely legs. Hers were no exception. We arrived home in time to catch the late news. Karolina's dropping jaw and shaking head only served to make Isabella's video clips all the more absurd. We settled in for the night by drinking coffee and trying to convince one another that our problems were over.

Isabella was a firecracker looking for a place to explode. She'd definitely found one in the form of the local PD. The only thing wrong was that it could explode on us first before Isabella managed to catch up to the dirty cops.

"I'm thinking Randy can't be too happy with what's going on. His little kingdom has been falling apart since I rode into town and got tangled up with you."

"Let's go to bed and talk about it," Karolina said. It wasn't a suggestion.

We abandoned any pretense of talking minutes after tearing off our clothes and kicking away the sheets. The instant the lights went out, more pounding echoed on the tin and into the trailer. It was like someone had been peering into the bedroom window waiting for the fun and games to begin. This time, both of us were forced to endure the absurdity of the local PD's incompetence as they stormed into the trailer.

They permitted us to get dressed before leading us, handcuffed and in chains, into the back of a van. We were unceremoniously tossed inside. The door slammed and we were driven off.

It wasn't the short ride to town I'd become accustomed to. After going from smooth pavement to bouncing dirt road, the vehicle slowed and then stopped. A rattling gate opened, the van drove past, and then past another gate and we were in a lighted yard. The compound was surrounded by steel fence topped with razor wire. What looked to be structures in a huge prison complex towered over us.

"I guess this is where we say goodbye. How long do you think it will be before Isabella finds us?"

A guard smacked a nightstick against the

palm of his hand. "No talking. Eyes straight ahead."

"I don't know, Frank, but I'm thinking she's going to make a pile of money thanks to us," Karolina said. For her trouble, Karolina ended up on the ground. She twitched and screamed as pain twisted her face. She managed to look up at me through slitted eyes.

"See what I mean? Big money. When she doesn't get a response to her text, I'm thinking she'll be right back with the Feds."

Karolina was right, although it took Isabella some bit of time to locate us. She dutifully showed up at the prison and loaded us into her Cadillac. Neither Karolina nor I asked any questions. We were exhausted, mentally and physically, from the week-long ordeal.

On the drive back to town, Isabella filled us in on what she'd been doing since we were imprisoned illegally, among other things on her laundry list of crimes committed against us. It wasn't pretty.

"Things have been happening in the background since my videos went live. The local mayor and council has been removed from office. Everyone on the local PD has been relieved of duty. The state police have replaced them temporarily."

Which was all right by any measure of accountability, but- "So what's a poor boy and girl to do?"

"Well, you can't go back to your place, Karolina. It's been torched." Isabella looked across at me.

"Your bike went up along with it, Frank. Fortunately, after the local fire department refused to respond, a souvenir video surfaced taken by a compadre. It shows one of them tossing a couple of Molotov cocktails through the windows of Karolina's trailer."

When that happened, we were on our way to prison. "Just as well we ended up in prison."

"You both have horseshoes nailed to your asses. Are you having any trouble sitting down with those lumps?" Isabella laughed.

"That can't be true, and you know it, Isabella. You've seen our asses. And I know for sure I don't clank when I sit down. I can't speak for Frank. All I can do is get him to lie down."

Isabella blushed and I smiled and Karolina laughed and then we all laughed at the absurdity of all of it.

It was the only thing left for us to do.

Isabella loaded us into her Cadillac and drove us into Phoenix. She convinced us to allow her to put us up until things quieted down. We were witness to her television appearances where she made out like a bandit. Even some dimwitted television lawyer had her on, not to mention the morning shows.

Our names weren't mentioned once, which was fine by me.

With my bike destroyed in the conflagration at Karolina's trailer, I poured over the papers and the bike shop adverts looking for another 95 bagger. I found one after about a week of looking.

I convinced Isabella to drop us off and I did a test ride with Karolina. The owner followed on another bike. He recognized us as the pair of desperadoes who'd brought down a police department all by our lonesome.

Karolina started right in telling him about Isabella. I stopped her before she got too carried away, explaining that you can never tell these days who's recording and who isn't. "He doesn't need to know about that," I told her.

She quieted down, although she looked disappointed, as though the wind had been let out of her sails.

Satisfied that the bike seemed to be in good mechanical shape, I headed off to a bank with the owner where I dished out the cash. Now all I needed was an address and I'd end up plated in Arizona—which wasn't a problem for Isabella. She had me fixed up in no time.

"We need to find a place of our own, Isabella. Until this all shakes out, we're going to be in demand by just about everyone from the state, the feds, and the rest of the losers back in bumwad, A-Zee."

Karolina nodded in agreement. Isabella looked at us like we were crazy. "Why wouldn't you stay here? It's got a great view. Plenty of security down in the lobby. It's close to trendy downtown. What more could you two want?"

"You're too kind, Isabella, and I'm really grateful. Without you, I'd be stuck in Valle Verde looking for another place. Frank would probably be out of my life, having already put up with enough trouble to last a lifetime."

"I know, but—"

Karolina held up a hand. "You're single. Picture a month of sharing your place with the two of us. You'd end up changing the locks and tossing us into the street just to be rid of us."

Finally, Isabella agreed, and I got the feeling she knew it to be true. "I know a guy. Let me make some phone calls for you."

Neither of us wanted charity. Isabella located a place out by Chandler. We agreed on a monthly rate for the furnished apartment. It was more than Karolina bargained for. She broke out in tears when I unlocked the door and she got a look at the inside. "I could never afford a place like this, Frank. Never in a million years."

The place was a little much with the

modern furniture and the view out the window and the neighborhood, but it was free. Who would say no to that?

"In that case, you better sign up at the local college and find a rich frat boy. In no time you'll be beating them off with a stick."

"At long as I'm not beating them off with my hand-" She grinned before leading me into the bedroom. I was only a little disappointed when she immediately began stripping the bed. She threw the sheets into the washer. "Better safe than sorry. Now let's go for groceries."

"You don't want to eat out?"

"With a place like this begging for two people to share dinner over candlelight? I don't think so, fella."

We loaded the bagger with groceries and headed for home. We hauled our treasures inside, and Karolina set out making what she called a romantic dinner for two. I eased up to the washer, hauled out the sheets, and put them in to dry. While she was in the shower, I made up the huge California king.

With nothing else to do, I headed for the shower.

"Out," she ordered. "I need to get dressed without having you around to distract me."

I hung my head and sheepishly headed for the kitchen. I set the table and waited. And waited. And waited. "Are you alive in there?"

Karolina halted at the door to the

bedroom. She hadn't brought much with her, but what she managed to pick up when I was doing the grocery shopping was good enough for me. She was beautiful in a short skirt and sheer blouse. The plain-looking woman with the flat tire I met at the gas pump was almost unrecognizable. "No wonder your friend Randy doesn't want to let you go."

"You already know why, biker boy. You can come back to the bedroom now. I put a hold on the candlelight. Supper won't be for a while."

We took our time. Pillow talk ran out when Karolina suggested we head farther north to get away from her ex. I let her know I'd consider it, but for now we'd be stuck where we were until Isabella didn't need us any more.

"If we're going to go ahead with a lawsuit, we might as well wait it out. We'll have plenty of time to figure out where we're going later."

The woman went all pouty on me. She didn't appear too happy knowing I wouldn't be jumping on the go train just because she wanted me to. It seemed like she got over it after a bit of food and a lot of wine.

Karolina's even breathing told me she was still sleeping. I had to be at a meeting with Isabella first thing. I rummaged through the dresser, searching for anything I had left that was clean. Impatient and in a hurry, I opened one of the drawers Karolina used. It fell out of the track and crashed to the floor. Her underwear scattered at the foot of the dresser. A plastic-wrapped package lay on the floor next to her underwear.

My breath caught. I slid the drawer back in place and scooped up the package. I checked on Karolina. She was still asleep. I deposited the twin packages on the dining room table. The dishes were still in place after we eagerly deserted the kitchen for the bedroom.

It wasn't easy to admit, but at least now I knew why she brought up wanting to head farther north. She had used Randy, her ex, as an excuse. More miles meant more money for the bundles of coca she had stashed with her underwear. I knew all about it from a bad experience a couple of years back.

In the darkened bedroom I quietly packed my belongings and headed for the door. Karolina was still breathing normally. I loaded up and beat a hasty retreat to Isabella's place. Her lights were on. I rang and she buzzed me in.

I wasted no time explaining why I needed to be heading out of town, and fast. I let her in on Karolina's secret. That she was a drug mule had taken me by surprise more than I wanted to admit to anyone—even Isabella.

"Are you sure, Frank? You just want to ride

off into the sunset and leave it all behind? You'll get quite a payday when it comes due. I will too, of course."

"I know, Isabella. But I didn't foresee anything like this. I think I need some road time to consider my next step."

She knew I wouldn't be held back. She knew me too well.

"Besides, you have more than enough on your plate with your own abduction and side trip into the desert. You're lucky to be alive."

"I already found a good lawyer friend I trust to represent me. I was hoping it would allow me to dedicate all of my time to your case. You'll end up with enough money to do whatever you want for the rest of your life."

I looked out the window and across the bright city lights stretching out in front of me like a magic carpet. It was way too big for my liking. Too easy to like.

"You know, I'm already doing that," I told her. "I have to count the small change, but it's hassle-free. And I can come and go as I please. When I want. How I want."

I knew she'd have an answer.

"Until it isn't. You already know what that's like. And Karolina shouldn't have any bearing on the treatment you endured by dirty cops, Frank."

"You're right, but all I want to do is get out of town. I'm sure if Karolina needs your help, she'll get in touch. If I were you, I wouldn't hold your breath. She was using both of us."

I said my goodbyes and walked out to my ride. I fired up and headed for a diner I once knew in another life. I took a seat at the counter and ordered the breakfast I would need to put the miles and my troubles in the rearview.

I waited it out, and twilight came soon enough. I paid up and headed out to my ride.

It was a good day to ride.

The desert air was just cool enough for a light jacket and gloves. I slipped on a comfortably faded, worn jacket to keep the cold off that I knew the fresh morning air would bring out on the highway. My tie-downs looked good. There was nothing worse than something falling off that I might need down the road.

I tied my bandana and checked it. I'd be able to pull it over my lower face in an instant if blowing sand or dust looked like it might interrupt the highway.

I punched the starter and Isabella showed up just as the bike began its throaty idle. "I knew you'd be here. I like the place, too. So long, Frank. I'll keep in touch." She knew I hated goodbyes.

"Thanks for everything. I'll be seeing you."

I reached the city's outskirts in time to

witness the early morning sunrise turn the gray, pre-dawn sky into a bright blue. The desert temperature was down. The humidity was up slightly. A biker in the wind would be just about right until high-noon desert heat took over.

I already knew the two-lane asphalt ribbon stretching out in front of me would lead head-on to friends and strangers and an adventure I hadn't yet experienced. If I ended up fortunate, maybe I'd cross paths with a long-haired, tight-bodied hitch-hiker. Or maybe a traveling woman riding her own looking for a little company. A man can't ask for much more than that.

It definitely was a good day to ride.

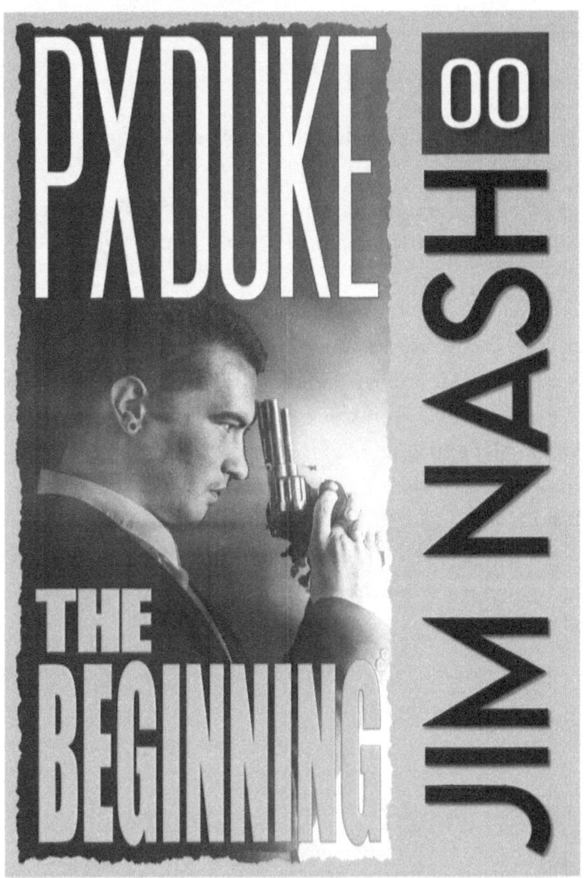

If you enjoyed reading about Frank Ross, you might like another PX Duke series. Police Detective Jim Nash has a murky back-story in the police department of a major city. Check it out.

About the author

Peter Duke is a Canadian author. He resides and writes in a small college town in Southern Ontario.

Aviator. Motorcycle rider. Vagabond. Drifter. Trouble-maker. Jack of all trades and master of none. Peter Duke has been riding and writing about the places he's been and the people he's seen for a few years now. Some of his writing is factual; some of it isn't. He likes to leave it up to his readers to decide for themselves which lies are the truth.

https://pxduke.com

peterxduke@gmail.com

9 781928 161691